Emma flashed Matt Suede what she hoped was a seductive smile. She leaned into his hug and became distracted by the playful dusting of freckles frolicking over his nose and across his cheeks.

Matt bent his head, whispering in for a kiss.

Emma pressed two fingers to his lips, preventing what promised to be a fascinating experience.

"Matt, honey, you did promise me a proper wedding. I don't think we should keep the preacher waiting."

Matt's arm stiffened. His fingers cramped about her middle. There was a very good chance that he had quit breathing.

The marshal let out a deep-bellied laugh that startled poor Pearl and made her whinney. "Looks like you been caught after all, Suede."

* * *

Renegade Most Wanted
Harlequin® Historical #1095—July 2012

Author Note

I have always been fascinated by the stories and the people of the Old West. Homesteaders in particular were a resilient lot who worked hard to build their homes and raise their families. My great-grandmother was one of them. She left behind the special gift of her memoirs.

She echoes through the pages of *Renegade Most Wanted*. You will find her in both our heroine, Emma, and her friend Rachael. Like Emma, my great-grandmother was a homesteader, and sold patent medicine for the relief of "female complaints." Like Rachael, she was a preacher.

I am thrilled to bring you Emma Parker and her outlaw cowboy, Matt Suede. Come along with them while they wrench their love, their family and their home from the stubborn Kansas prairie.

I hope you enjoy reading this story as much as I have enjoyed writing it.

You may contact me at carolsarens@yahoo.com.

Warm wishes!

RENEGADE MOST WANTED

CAROL ARENS

HARLEQUIN®
entertain, enrich, inspire™

Recycling programs
for this product may
not exist in your area.

ISBN-13: 978-0-373-29695-8

RENEGADE MOST WANTED

Copyright © 2012 by Carol Arens

All rights reserved. Except for use in any review, the reproduction or utilization of this work in whole or in part in any form by any electronic, mechanical or other means, now known or hereafter invented, including xerography, photocopying and recording, or in any information storage or retrieval system, is forbidden without the written permission of the publisher, Harlequin Enterprises Limited, 225 Duncan Mill Road, Don Mills, Ontario, Canada M3B 3K9.

This is a work of fiction. Names, characters, places and incidents are either the product of the author's imagination or are used fictitiously, and any resemblance to actual persons, living or dead, business establishments, events or locales is entirely coincidental.

This edition published by arrangement with Harlequin Books S.A.

For questions and comments about the quality of this book please contact us at Customer_eCare@Harlequin.ca.

® and TM are trademarks of Harlequin Enterprises Limited or its corporate affiliates. Trademarks indicated with ® are registered in the United States Patent and Trademark Office, the Canadian Trade Marks Office and in other countries.

www.Harlequin.com

Printed in U.S.A.

While in the third grade, **Carol Arens** had a teacher who noted that she ought to spend less time daydreaming and looking out of the window and more time on her sums. Today, Carol spends as little time on sums as possible. Daydreaming about plots and characters is still far more interesting to her.

As a young girl, she read books by the dozen. She dreamed that one day she would write a book of her own. A few years later Carol set her sights on a new dream. She wanted to be the mother of four children. She was blessed with a son, then three daughters. While raising them she never forgot her goal of becoming a writer. When her last child went to high school she purchased a big old clunky word processor and began to type out a story.

She joined Romance Writers of America, where she met generous authors who taught her the craft of writing a romance novel. With the knowledge she gained, she sold her first book and saw her lifelong dream come true.

Carol lives with her real-life hero and husband, Rick, in Southern California, where she was born and raised. She feels blessed to be doing what she loves, with all her children and a growing number of perfect and delightful grandchildren living only a few miles from her front door.

When she is not writing, reading or playing with her grandchildren, Carol loves making trips to the local nursery. She delights in scanning the rows of flowers, envisaging which pretty plants will best brighten her garden.

She enjoys hearing from readers, and invites you to contact her at carolsarens@yahoo.com.

Available from Harlequin® Historical and CAROL ARENS

*Scandal at the Cahill Saloon

*Part of the Cahil Cowboys continuity

With love to my husband, Rick.
Cheers to thirty-six years!

Chapter One

Dodge City, Kansas, 1881

Land sakes! What did a woman have to do to get a husband in this cowboy-thick town—dance naked on the back of a steer?

Emma Parker licked a film of dust from her lips to make them look moist and alluring, but it was no use. She had been perched upon the bench outside the land office for so long that the wind, a perverse thing that spared no regard for a woman's appearance, had spun her into a mound of bedraggled frippery.

No wonder the men passing by paid her no mind. July sunshine burned down like a blister to complete the ruination of her gown. Damp pink taffeta clung to her throat while a hank of droopy lace sagged against her bosom. Truly, what had ever made her think to spend a years' worth of egg money on the ineffective garment?

A drip of perspiration trickled between her breasts, not unlike the disturbing sensation of a spider skittering over her skin. Mercy, for a dime she'd take a plunge into the Arkansas River flowing south of town, new dress be hanged.

There might have been a cooler, less dirt-ridden part of town to seek a spouse, but the men here kept up a constant coming and going. Not a moment passed that one didn't come out of the mercantile or go into the saloon. This ought to have been as easy as plucking peaches from a tree.

To bolster her spirits, Emma touched her breast where a letter from a former employer was folded between her skin and the lace of her shift. She no longer needed to see the letter in order to read it. Every word was memorized, burned into her heart, giving life to her dreams.

"'Dear Emma,'" she recited in a whisper. "'We find that we must move on in haste. Our wonderful homestead, a pure piece of paradise, will be free for the taking. We know how you yearn for a home of your own. Time is not on your side, dear. Catch the first train to Dodge before some other lucky soul files on it. May your future return to you all the joy and kindness that you have shown to our children over the years. Please do come quickly. Edna Harkins.'"

So far she had been lucky. The former Harkins place had not been filed on. It was destined to be hers, even if she had to flirt with every last bachelor in Dodge to get it.

Emma watched a prospective groom rumble down the earthen street in his wagon. Her loveliest smile earned no more than a raised hat when he rolled past. Drat if the jingle of his harness didn't sound as if it was laughing at her.

This rough splintered bench should have been the

perfect spot to catch a man. She couldn't imagine what she was doing wrong. Weren't the men of the west desperate for helpful mates? She'd always heard that was true, but her efforts at appearing irresistible seemed to be falling flat.

She'd bet a pretty penny that the man in the wagon would have no trouble at all filing a claim. His gender alone would make it a simple thing.

Pinpricks of irritation plucked at her patience. She wouldn't even need a husband if the politicians who had passed the Homestead Act had been more open-minded about the rules. Even the clerk in the land office acted as if he had written them himself, the way he stuck to the very letter of the law.

Earlier this morning she had explained until her voice had grown hoarse that she was an orphan and no one knew her true age.

"The law says you've got to be twenty-one or head of a household. Even if guessing were allowed, you don't look to be more than twenty." The clerk scratched the lower of his double chins and wagged his finger at her. "Besides, I don't see what a pretty little thing like you is going to do with all that land. No sir, it doesn't seem safe or proper."

And when had her life ever been safe or proper? The homestead was the one thing that would give her that. On her own land she'd put down deep roots where life's whims couldn't blow her about.

"As you'll recall," Emma had said, gathering her patience, "I do have—"

"Don't tell me again that your blind horse qualifies you to be head of a household. You've got to have a young'un for that."

That male-thinking nonsense curdled her stomach.

Since adopting a young'un was the very last thing she intended to do, she was stuck with finding a head of the household to file her claim for her. Anyone still breathing would do. After all, they would be married only the few moments it would take the gent to file her claim. The lucky man would then walk away ten dollars richer.

Heavy boot thumps drummed the wooden sidewalk. Emma twirled her dainty satin parasol and glanced to her left with a wide blink and a smile that felt like yesterday's flowers.

A tall man, a dandy by the looks of him, blew a ring of cigarette smoke into the fleeting afternoon. He strode past her with his back stiff and his polished boots reflecting arrows of sunlight.

The stench of stale cologne and nicotine trailed behind him long after he disappeared through the land-office doo...

What if the stick-to-the-letter-of-the-law clerk issued the dandified gent the claim to the homestead that she had traveled hundreds of miles by clackety, bone-jarring train to stake as her own? Her mind saw the transaction occurring as clearly as if the building had no walls.

Emma groaned, then glanced across the street through a gap between a pair of buildings. The sun had already begun its long red slide toward a horizon that looked like the end of the earth itself.

Somewhere on that flat, golden prairie was her new home. She intended to sleep there tonight, to listen to the wind blow over her very own grass. In the morning she would wake to a chorus of birds singing about her shining new future.

Emma redoubled her efforts to attract the attention of a farmer crossing the street only a few yards from where she sat. He stepped into the mercantile without so much as a tipped hat.

"Good morning, Mr. Pendragon." Emma heard an adolescent voice greet the stiff-postured gentleman who had just stepped inside the land office. "Good day for a bank robbery."

"There will be no holdup today, boy," a cultured voice snapped. "I've taken precautions this time."

A redheaded youth stepped outside with a broom gripped in his fists. He shoved it back and forth across the boardwalk with a swish and sway.

The boy paused in his sweeping to nod at her. "You sit there long enough, ma'am, and you'll see The Ghost."

Emma didn't want to see a ghost—she wanted to see a willing man. Too bad this boy attacking the dust on the walk was so young.

What had to be Mr. Pendragon's voice—sounding peeved—carried out of the land-office door. "There is no ghost, young sir! It's merely a thief determined to get his neck stretched."

The boy stopped sweeping and leaned against the broom handle. He gazed down the sidewalk, past the mercantile toward the bank.

"He's a thief, all right," he muttered to Emma. "The money's always good and gone. But he's no mortal bank robber—anyone will say so."

"They will?" Emma asked, trying to ignore the sun slipping another notch toward the horizon.

"There's a ghost and it's a fact." The boy resumed his sweeping, stirring up a swell of dust that settled on her eyelashes and tickled her nose.

"I expect even The Ghost is married," Emma mumbled.

"Beg pardon, ma'am?"

"Never mind. What makes you so certain the bank will be robbed today?"

The boy sat down beside her on the bench. He lowered his voice to a confidential whisper.

"That fellow inside, Mr. Pendragon, got paid on a load of cattle he shipped east. Made a big deposit to the bank this morning." He nodded toward the doorway of the land office. "The Ghost only robs Mr. Pendragon."

"How considerate." She tapped her toe on the boardwalk. Time was quickly becoming her enemy. "Mr. Pendragon sounds like an English gentleman."

"He's someone lordly. Got a huge spread outside of town. Each week he sends in one of his hands to take up homesteads on the deserted places all around. Before long, nobody will have a steer that doesn't graze on Pendragon land."

Emma's heart dropped and spun around. A less purposeful woman might have felt a ladylike swoon coming on.

Lands! She needed a husband. If she didn't get one quickly, Pendragon would snatch up her homestead!

Apparently finished with ghost tales, the boy got up and went back inside the land office.

Emma snatched her shotgun from her lap and tucked it under her skirt, leaving only a few inches of the barrel in view. Maybe that's what was scaring the gents away. They wouldn't know it was unloaded and that she had never fired more than a pebble at a rat in the henhouse. It wouldn't be wise to let it go completely unseen in a half-settled cow town like Dodge, but surely she looked more sociable now.

After twenty minutes of smiling like the dickens and quietly cursing under her breath, Emma stood up to regain the circulation in her backside. She shook the dust from her parasol and brushed up a cloud of it from her skirt. Lord only knew what the palms of her frilly white gloves would look like when she was finished.

After what seemed an eternity, the Englishman strutted out of the land office and blew out a lungful of smoke. He flicked the butt of his cigarette on the sidewalk, then ground it out with his boot heel.

"You'll make sure my man gets that piece of property?" he called back inside.

Emma didn't hear the answer, but it must have been yes, for a smug grin shot over his narrow jaw before he lurched into a buggy and drove his team out of town down Front Street.

It must be her land he had spoken of! Surely it was, since the place was said to be no less than paradise on earth. What other piece of ground could he have wanted?

With her heart flip-flopping in her chest, Emma rushed through the land-office doorway. She stomped toward the clerk lounging at his desk.

Drat, she hadn't noticed that she had led the way with her shotgun until the boy dropped his broom. It clattered like scattered marbles on the floor.

The clerk choked on a swallow of something that he had raised to his lips in a ruby-colored glass. She was unlikely to win any favors from the man now.

"Was that my land he wanted?" She tried to sound like sweetness and light, but it was no good. She pointed the nose of the gun toward the floor. "It's not actually loaded."

A pair of relieved sighs whooshed through the office.

"Well, now, Miss Parker." The land-office manager tipped back in his chair and folded his hands across his wide belly. "Unless you've turned twenty-one or become the head of a household since you came in this morning, I can't give you that homestead."

"Did the Englishman take it?"

"No, miss, he wanted another."

"Praise be!" Emma spun about and fairly skipped out the door, her hope renewed. The expensive lace border on her dress caught Mr. Pendragon's discarded cigarette ashes like the best of brooms. Her gown was getting grayer by the hour. Unless she found a man soon she'd be the dingiest bride to ever wed in Dodge.

She resumed her seat on the bench, fluffed her withered skirt and set her smile in place. In spite of the obstacles Dodge City had thrown in her way, she would catch a husband, and she would do it today.

Days didn't come along much finer than this one. Matt Suede tugged his hat brim down to shade his eyes from the afternoon sun. His boot heels clicking on the boardwalk echoed up and down Front Street.

Town was quiet this time of day, with the morning's business completed and the evening's not yet begun, just the way it suited him, but something felt wrong.

He ought to pay attention to that niggling feeling. The smart thing would be to call off the bank robbery for today. Then again, it would be his last holdup and he'd like to get it over with.

A dust devil whirled down the middle of the street. A

woman sitting on a bench outside the land office swung up her parasol, hiding from the gust until it passed by.

Matt slowed his pace. The lady was something to look at, as appealing as a prairie flower. She shook dust from her umbrella, then fluffed her skirt out on the bench.

Her hair had mostly come undone from the bun at her neck. Sunlight speckled gold threads in the curls that tumbled down her back.

When he had the time he'd have to remember her delicate womanhood and make up a song about her. He'd sing it to the beeves to soothe them at roundup some long dark night from now.

He might have approached her if his plans for the afternoon had been different, but he shouldn't have slowed his pace as it was.

He'd passed by the marshal's office and been relieved to see Dodge's lawman asleep. His snorts and snores should have been reassuring, but the air was ripe with something being wrong.

Matt glanced up and down the street, ready to duck behind the building where his cousin and accomplice, Billy, waited with a getaway horse in a gully covered with brush. There was just enough space between overgrowth and sand to hide a man and a horse, but not for long.

He'd just made up his mind to sneak around back when Gray Derby Bart, the meanest drunk in Dodge, staggered up to the woman on the bench. She smiled at him politely, but she had no idea what she might be getting into just by that common act of friendliness.

Bart might be a small man but he was mean through and through, especially when it came to the gentler sex.

Matt quick-footed it past the bank. Billy could wait a few minutes. The woman could not.

The sky at sunrise wasn't as pretty as her blue eyes. From the spark of interest glittering in Bart's rheumy gaze, he must have thought the same, but not in any respectful way a man should look at a decent woman.

"Afternoon, ma'am...Bart?" Matt tipped his hat. The lady turned her smile away from Bart and let it shine on him. Chilly nights on the cow trail would be considerably warmer if he could remember her smile, just so.

"Good afternoon." Her voice washed clean through him. It was the sweetest sound he'd heard in some time.

"I hope Bart here isn't causing you any concern, miss."

"My concern ain't no concern of yours, Matthew Suede." Bart's lip curled up in one corner, like an old dog snapping for a fight. "Me and the lady were conducting some personal business."

Sometimes when he was in his cups Bart imagined things. This sure would be one of those times, since this delicate woman would not be likely to have dealings with a scoundrel.

Matt dug into his pocket and withdrew a dollar bill. He pushed it into Bart's fist. "Go on over to the Long Branch and give that business some further thought."

Bart glanced at the money, then at the lady. Oddly enough, she didn't seem pleased. Surely she couldn't be sorry to be rid of Bart.

"I'll be back shortly, sweet thing. You wait right here for me and we'll finish what we were up to." Bart closed one eye in a lewd wink. A dribble of spit leaked out the corner of his mouth when he leaned forward as though he thought to kiss the lady.

She snapped her umbrella up. Such a frilly weapon wouldn't discourage that snake. The lady wouldn't know not to make an enemy of Bart. Best to keep him pointed toward the saloon and let him drink his meanness into a stupor.

"Go on, now." Matt stepped between the parasol and the drunk. He directed Bart down the steps much as he would herd a straying cow. "Bad luck to let good whiskey go waiting."

"Don't you move, sweet thing," Bart called from halfway across the street.

From behind, a rustling of silk and lace told Matt that the woman had risen from the bench. He'd like to stay a while and bask in her gratitude for getting rid of Bart, but Billy was probably getting nervous by now.

If the day had been different he would have invited the lady for a steak at Del Monico's. They could get acquainted in a proper way.

"Blast and tarnation!"

Startled, Matt spun about and found himself gazing down at the woman's shifting bustle. Too soon she straightened, then whirled on him with a shotgun gripped in her small, lacy-gloved fists.

This rose had thorns all up and down her pretty stem.

"Why, you interfering do-gooder!" She must have seen him go wide-eyed, for she plunked her weapon, nose-first, onto the boardwalk. "I was just about to get a—"

All of a sudden her gaze turned speculative. She slid the shotgun onto the bench behind her along with her umbrella. She planted her hands on her hips, swaying ever so slightly while she looked him up and down. Now he knew how a steer would feel, being priced for market.

All of a sudden the woman appeared soft, like a cuddly kitten that had retracted its claws.

"You stay clear of that old man, miss. He may not look like much, but he's mean as a mad dog."

Matt spun about. It was definitely time to meet his cousin.

"Mr. Suede," he heard the lady call out from behind. "Are you a married man?"

He glanced back, smiled and tipped his hat, but his boots couldn't carry him down the walk fast enough.

Emma pushed open the door to the livery and stepped inside. A beam of light from a window near the rafters stabbed through the interior of the huge barn, making it feel almost like church on a quiet afternoon. If it hadn't been for the dust particles swirling lazily about, she'd have been of a mind to get on her knees and ask the almighty for a man. But she'd had about enough of dust for one day. The livery floor, while clean enough for a barn, wasn't the place to kneel in a prolonged prayer, and prolonged prayer was what she would need to get a husband before the land office closed for the day.

"Mr. Adams?" Emma called out.

Jesse Adams kept his livery as neat as a woman kept a house. It smelled good in here, with the scent of polished leather, fresh hay and clean horses all mixed together.

A door in the back of the barn creaked open. A man poked his head through the opening but didn't come inside. From a dim corner a horse nickered a greeting.

"Oh…good afternoon, Miss Parker." Jesse Adams took a glance back at whatever he had been doing, then flashed a fresh, friendly grin at her. Too bad the man claimed to be nearly engaged. "Is there something I can help you with?"

"I've just come by to check on my horse and my supplies. Do you mind if I stay here for a while?"

A frown creased his forehead while he considered her request but he said, "You make yourself at home, ma'am. I'll be right out back. Holler if you need something."

If only hollering would get her what she needed. She'd come so close, too. That old gent in front of the mercantile had all but agreed to marry her, and for only ten dollars. True, he had been drunk and smelly, but she could have overlooked those flaws for the few moments she would need to borrow his name.

Drat that fine-looking Mr. Suede. If he hadn't filled her prospect's fist with money and sent him along to the saloon, she'd be hitching up her rented team, ready to cross the wide-open prairie by now. She'd finally be going home.

Not to someone else's home, to her own. What a wonder it would be to plant trees in her own soil and watch them grow. Wouldn't it be fine to not have to continually move on, and leave her plantings to grow up without her?

In her new life there wouldn't be other people's children hanging on her skirts wanting this and that. Emma had still been a child herself when she had started raising other folks' babies. Praise be that the days of other people's children were behind her. No more wiping runny noses, sitting up all night through fevers and cheering their first steps and words, just to be forced to take another position and never see them again.

From now on it was just Emma, free to come and

go, free to sit or stand, with nobody wanting a thing from her.

Emma watched the rectangle of light grow dark when Jesse closed the barn door. She turned about and walked with open arms toward her horse.

"Well, Pearl, old girl." Pearl wasn't really old, but she was blind and tended to move with caution, which gave her an aged look. Emma stroked the velvety nose that nudged her ribs in welcome. "I missed you, too. There's just a little chance that you'll have to spend the night at the livery one more time. Seems like the men here are a bit skittish when it comes to matrimony. It's not at all like everyone back in Indiana says."

No indeed, it was so much more complicated getting a husband. She had expected to simply file on the land that Edna Harkins had written her about and gone to live on a piece of earth that would be her own.

She hadn't figured on the trials of having to get a man. Well, that was just one more complication of having been an orphan. Being left on the steps of a church as a newborn had made her who she was, for good and for ill.

Emma rubbed Pearl behind one ear, then patted the white diamond on the chestnut head before she went to the corner of the livery where her rented wagon stood ready and waiting to make the trip to her homestead.

"Don't you worry, Pearl, we'll go home soon," Emma called out to the horse while she lifted the flap covering the goods necessary to set up housekeeping. She had passed the morning at various shops in Dodge using an uncomfortable portion of her savings, but she had spent wisely and had the funds to get started and then some.

Emma touched the bag of money tied about her

waist. It couldn't be seen beneath her skirt, but when she walked, it hit her thigh with a reassuring slap.

Very soon, life would be grander than she could have ever imagined. Those days of caring for everyone but herself were at an end. Poor orphan Emma, whom everyone pitied enough to take into their home in exchange for working her youth away, was about to become queen of her world.

"This time tomorrow, Pearl, you'll be grazing on land so nice and flat and big that you can wander about all day and never leave home."

Poor blind Pearl—Emma hoped that the horse would enjoy the freedom of the open country. Years ago an employer had given her the horse as a parting gift when he had decided to move his family to the East Coast. Families came and went, but Pearl was her own.

With a sigh, she put away misty memories of children that were not her own and trees that grew tall without her.

The troublesome search for a husband had done her in. Surely she would have better luck after she was fresh and rested. Just behind her rented wagon was a clean heap of straw that would do for a short nap. She lay down on it, spread her arms wide and watched dust specks play tag in a beam of light.

Wasn't this fine? To simply lie back without an employer needing this or that seemed the life of luxury.

Just as soon as she borrowed a man, life would be cherries and cream.

Emma came awake to the urgent whispers of two men behind the livery. As the pleasant fuzziness of her nap cleared from her mind, she recognized one voice as that of Jesse Adams.

She sat up, then heard running bootsteps pounding outside, following the sidewall of the livery. They made a skidding turn, then dashed inside.

The wagon, loaded with her supplies, prevented her from seeing who the running boots belonged to, but she heard the quick rush of a man's winded breathing.

His feet shuffled in the dirt and then three white stockings came flying over the wagon. They whooshed past her face and drifted down onto her straw bed.

She snatched them up. The livery filled with shouting male voices, one deep voice barking out over the rest for order.

"Look what we've got here, boys," the deep voice said. Emma scrunched low on her bed of straw, lying flat on her belly to peer through the spokes of the wagon wheels.

One pair of motionless boots faced half a dozen pair that shuffled up dust on the livery floor.

With seven men in the livery, odds were fair that at least one of them was a single man.

"Afternoon, Marshal Deeds," said the owner of the pair of boots facing the others.

"Afternoon, Suede. You happen to see a ghost run in here?" Deep guffaws followed the marshal's question.

A ghost? Emma opened the stockings wadded up in her fists. Yes, indeed, a ghost. Her fingers popped right through the cut-out eyeholes of one of the scraps.

"You been drinking on the job, Marshal?"

"Mighty funny, Matt, that The Ghost comes flying into the livery and here you happen to be, all alone." This voice came from the back of the gathering of boots.

Lands! That handsome Mr. Suede who had sent her drunk prospect packing was a bank robber? He'd seemed such a decent sort. Perhaps there was some personal grudge between Mr. Pendragon and…The Ghost, since the dandy was the only one who got robbed.

"It's no crime to be in the livery."

"Give it up, Suede. Everyone here saw you run inside."

The boots belonging to the marshal took a step forward. Matt Suede's boots didn't move a piece of grit out of place.

"I'm going to have to arrest you, Suede."

"Pendragon's going to see that you hang," the owner of a pair of boots with a rip in one toe said. "You might have ate your last meal and not even known it."

Mercy! Just when things seemed darkest, life always seemed to take a bright turn.

Emma opened the first button of her bodice, glanced down to judge the effect, then opened three more. For good measure she stuffed in a hank of straw. Hopefully her eyes still had a sleepy, languid look from her nap. A few more pieces of straw would be just the thing. She snatched them up, poked them into her hair, then mussed the whole thing with her fingertips.

She wadded up the stocking scraps and slowly, silently shoved them deep into the straw.

"Matt? Honey…" Emma stood up from the straw bed stretching and yawning like a cat full of cream. "Come on back here—you can check on poor blind Pearl later."

Matt Suede turned in a slow pivot. His manly jaw fell open. Earth-colored brows shot up over golden-brown eyes gone wide with surprise. Gradually his mouth closed, his grin stretched wide. Wrinkles creased the corners of eyes that seemed to be laughing in relief and mischief. Mostly mischief.

Emma stepped out from behind the wagon looking down and pretending to struggle with the buttons of her gown as though she hadn't noticed the men gawking at her.

"Button these back up for me, will you?" Did her hips sashay the right way? Appearing scandalous had never been among her best skills. "You're so much better at it than I—"

Emma looked up, gasped and covered her half-naked breasts with the splayed fingers of one hand.

"Lands! Matt, honey, who are these men?"

"The marshal." Matt Suede gripped her shoulders with firm, calloused hands. He inclined his head toward the body of men. "And his friends."

Matt stared down at her gaping bodice, then looked into her eyes. His brows rose in an expression that she could see, but not the men standing behind him. Clearly, he was seeking permission to complete the intimate task. With an infinite dip of her head she answered him. Yes.

"Don't you gentlemen know not to intrude on a private moment?" She tried to use a scolding voice, but Matt's rough-skinned knuckles brushed her chest when he slid a button home. Her voice sounded husky instead of incensed.

"They say they saw The Ghost fly into the barn," Matt said. Emma took a shaking breath and wished he would hurry with those buttons. She couldn't take her gaze off those brown, weathered fingers lingering on her flesh. Lands, the blush flooded her skin in heat waves. "They figure that since I'm the only man in here, I must be The Ghost."

"What foolishness," Emma declared, and straightened the collar of her now demurely buttoned gown. "I believe that if Matt were a spirit, I would have noticed some moments back." She inclined her head toward the rumpled pile of hay behind the wagon and plucked a blade of straw from her hair. "I'm quite sure this man is flesh and blood."

Evidently her declaration of his humanity pleased him, for a grin shot over his lightly bristled jaw. He swatted a hank of golden-brown hair back from his face and slipped his arm around her waist.

He seemed awfully relaxed. His arm made itself at home, snuggling against her back while his fingers stroked her ribs, petting as though they had done it a thousand times before.

Emma flashed Matt Suede what she hoped was a seductive smile. She leaned into his hug and became distracted by the playful dusting of freckles frolicking over his nose and across his cheeks.

Matt bent his head, whispering in for a kiss.

Emma pressed two fingers to his lips, preventing what promised to be a fascinating experience.

"Matt, honey, you did promise me a proper wedding. I don't think we should keep the preacher waiting."

Matt's arm stiffened, his fingers cramped about her middle. There was a very good chance that he had quit breathing.

The marshal let out a deep-bellied laugh that startled poor Pearl and made her whinny. "Looks like you been caught after all, Suede."

"If you ain't The Ghost, you can't deny being the groom," someone snickered.

"Since you don't see a spook standing here, I believe you're looking at the groom." Matt Suede's voice croaked on the word *groom*.

"The problem is, I don't recall you having a steady girl, Suede," the marshal said. "Just to be sure you and the lady here aren't in cahoots, I think the boys and I will just go along to witness those holy vows."

A man slapped his thigh and let out a roaring hoot. "Singing Trigger Suede goes through with this marriage and we'll know he's telling the truth."

"You've got the wrong bank robber, boys. The next hour will see me hitched and tied."

Matt bent his mouth close to her ear. His breath warmed her cheek.

"You sure you want to do this, ma'am?" he whispered. The men standing nearby wouldn't hear him, since they stood close to the barn door and the traffic traveling down Front Street drowned his words to anyone but her. "I'm better than that old drunk, but only a little."

Chapter Two

It's not that Matt had anything against married men. In fact, he judged that, largely, they were the lucky ones. He'd just never figured to be one of them. Not every man could live up to the responsibility.

He glanced down at the small gloved hand nestling in the crook of his elbow. The woman had saved him from the hangman's noose. He guessed he owed her for that and would have to go along with what she was up to, for now.

Even if he didn't owe her, when the choice was hang or wed, what was a neck-loving man to do?

It hadn't taken more than a couple of minutes for the marshal and his cohorts to hunt up Mrs. Sizeloff, a lay preacher who had just come down the bank steps. The marshal and five hooting witnesses demanded her immediate services as reverend. Since lay ministers were allowed to perform churchly duties, she had been whisked away to make sure he was wed.

It felt like a lynching more than a wedding, but the lady beside him didn't flinch. In fact, her smile looked brighter than the sun riding big and low in the western sky.

Now here they were, if not dearly beloved, at least gathered together in the land office. He'd gallantly pointed out that there was a church at the edge of town, but his bride had muttered something odd that sounded like the land office was getting ready to close.

In under a quarter of an hour his whole life had upended. Already the preacher was winding up to the big "I do."

Preacher Sizeloff spoke of living together in love and peace. Every soul in the land office had known Matt for years. Which one of them believed that Singing Trigger Suede had suddenly given his heart to the pretty newcomer to Dodge? He'd better act like a man smitten if he wanted to escape that noose.

When the reverend spoke about forsaking all others, Matt gulped. This was so permanent, so final, but what choice did he have but to turn his head and grin down at his bride as though that's just what he had been dreaming of, cleaving only to his wife?

Mrs. Sizeloff asked him to swear it before God and all these witnesses.

"I, Matthew Jonathan Suede, take you—" Who? Ma'am?

He was vowing to honor and cherish a woman whose name he didn't even know! Panic tripped his heart. The marshal would never believe he hadn't just met her a few moments ago in the livery.

His bride smiled brilliantly—it almost made him forget to breathe. She dabbed at her eye with a grimy white glove.

"Matt, honey," she said. "Aren't we a pair? My mama always said, Emma Parker, you're too emotional by half.

The only time you can't get out a word is when you're about to weep. Oh, Matt...I...I..."

All of a sudden Emma Parker hid her face in her hands and sobbed.

Matt lifted her chin and tried to peer past her fingers. He brushed her hands aside. Real tears rolled down her face, leaving dirty streaks from the dust on her gloves.

"It's all right, Emma darlin'." He stroked her cheeks to dry and clean them. "I do take you to be my wedded wife."

"I take you, too, Matt, to love and obey." Didn't her eyes look blue and sincere? He nearly believed her.

"Well, then..." Mrs. Sizeloff sighed and looked fondly upon them, hugged up tight together. She must believe it, as well. "I now pronounce you man and wife. Matt, you and your wife will need to come by the church and sign the marriage license, but for now, you may kiss the bride."

This was something he could do convincingly. Those pink lips had been setting off poetry in his mind ever since he'd first seen them, not an hour ago.

For an instant hesitation flashed in Emma's eyes, but he had to make this look good or those fools standing around with horse laughs breaking out on their faces would string him up.

He touched the curls at Emma Parker's temple while he dipped his head low. His bride had hair that felt like dove's feathers. Would she let him touch it again after this show was over?

Emma closed her eyes and puckered her mouth. He pressed his lips on the rosy, tense circle. He should probably pull away, let it end chaste and sweet, but a man didn't get married every day.

His blood began a slow swell, throbbing in his heart and lower. He pressed the kiss deeper and traced the crease of her mouth with his tongue.

Emma's lips parted in what must have been surprise. She tipped her head backward, opened her eyes and gazed at him. Did ever eyes shine so blue with bewilderment and delight?

This time, when he lowered his mouth, her lips opened without any coaxing. Damned if he could make himself lift his wind-worn mouth from her dewy one.

He might have gone on and on, and her going right along with him, if the marshal and the rest hadn't started to hoot and holler.

Ending that kiss forced a groan clear to parts unseen. His wife's mouth had done unholy things to his body, or maybe not unholy, after all, since they were now wed.

He looked at her face and, judging by the flush that crept from under her lace collar, she felt a call to the marriage bed as strongly as he did.

Before they set foot down that trail, he'd have to tell her that they couldn't cleave to one another as Mrs. Sizeloff had bound them to do.

There were things about him that she didn't know. Things wives had a right to know before the "I do's." Not the least of which was that a killer with revenge on his mind was getting out of prison.

Come summer's end, Angus Hawker would be a threat to everyone that Matt held dear.

Emma frowned at Matthew Jonathan Suede, sitting beside her on the wagon bench as if he were king of the prairie. He drove her rented team, holding the reins loose in his fingers while they rattled off toward the sunset and her new home. Apparently the man misunderstood the nature of their marriage.

Right after he'd filed her claim, she'd thanked him and bid him goodbye. She'd fairly skipped toward the livery and her new life, only to hear his boots thumping down the boardwalk after her. She'd offered him the ten dollars she had been willing to give the drunk, but he'd looked at her as though she had become suddenly feebleminded.

To her dismay, he'd followed her into the livery. The name she'd called him was probably uncalled for, but really, he'd tied poor blind Pearl and his own horse behind the wagon, then tossed her onto the plank seat as though she were no more than a stick of straw! He'd then climbed aboard, taken control of the driving and remained silent for the best part of an hour.

Silence was best. She took pleasure in watching the prairie grass roll past. She found joy in simply listening to the birds sing to the parting day. Way off in the west the sun slipped toward the long horizon like a ball of orange fire.

What a wide, wonderful land! Mercy, she didn't think she could breathe and smell and hear enough of it. If she lived on her little spot of paradise for a hundred years it wouldn't be long enough.

Evidently Mr. Suede couldn't resist the evening's beauty any more than she could. His shoulders went soft and a smile tugged at the corners of his mouth. His eyes, gazing out at the big empty land, became a mirror for the golden grass stretching out forever.

Then, with the birds chirruping out their last and the crickets just tuning up, Matt Suede began to sing.

He had a clear, low voice that shot straight to a person's heart. With the harness creaking and the horses' hooves keeping time, he sang a story about a man who got caught up in a stampede and died saving the life of his boss's daughter.

The soul-deep melody echoing over the twilight prairie was enough to make Emma want to weep... and forgive him. A cow, so far off that she couldn't see it, bawled out long and low, as though it, too, had been touched by the teary tale.

Emma shook herself. Mr. Suede was a bank robber. The roof of it, Mr. Suede's ghostly apparel, lay hidden beneath the extra corset stored in her trunk.

But mercy be! How could such a heavenly sound come out of a criminal? And there was that kiss! Surely she wouldn't have felt like a hot noodle under the lips of a villain. To be fair, he had acted gallantly when he'd shooed away the drunk she'd been about to marry. Thinking back on it, she realized the man might have been a problem.

At the very instant he quit singing, the sun passed below the horizon. Behind them a fat full moon swelled into the sky to light the dusk.

"I'm sorry I called you that name back at the livery." Her voice sounded like pebbles grinding together compared to the notes that had come from Matt Suede's throat. "It's just that I expected you to go on your way. I never meant that you really had to be my husband."

"Well, now, ma'am, I accept your apology." Matt clicked to the rented team when one of the horses decided to stop and munch on a tuft of grass. "And I thank you for saving my neck, but that was a real preacher and that marriage certificate does make us legally bound."

Emma's heart took a dive. What if her husband

leaned more to thievery than gallantry? If a body wanted to look at things strictly legally, whose name was on that claim?

Emma Laurel Parker...Suede, to be sure, but before hers was Matthew Jonathan Suede. She might be no better off than she had been sitting on the bench in front of the land office.

"I never meant for us to be bound, Mr. Suede. I only needed a husband so that I could file on my land and... well, to be honest, I knew you couldn't turn me down. But now I don't hold you to it. You're free to take your horse and ride off."

Emma gazed sidelong at him. He had slipped the hat back from his head. It hung down his back from a pair of strings that pulled across a red bandanna tied around his neck. His shoulder-length hair was a shade more golden than the rich soil they rolled over. Moon glow cast shifting light over him, gilding those golden-brown waves in shadow and sparkle.

If a woman did want to take on the care of a husband, Matt Suede would be a fine one to look at over the years. But the last thing Emma wanted was someone to take care of. In her new life, the only one wanting something from her would be her, and naturally, Pearl.

"You are a free man, Mr. Suede. I'll do just fine on my own."

"I see a pair of problems with your logic, ma'am. First problem is, I'm only a free man so long as the marshal believes that I didn't just meet you in the livery."

That's something she should have considered when she'd hitched her star to an outlaw cowboy.

"Looks like you've got yourself a loving husband for the time being."

"What's the other problem with my logic?"

"I can't quite figure out what a pretty little thing like you is going to do with a hundred and sixty acres of stubborn prairie sod. You don't look like any farmer I ever saw."

"I'll admit I look small, but I'm tough. If I had a mind to bust up sod, I would." Emma sat up taller, even though the lurching wagon made her rock back and forth as stiffly as a metronome. "As it happens, I intend to simply live on the land, just let it be mine."

"Back at the land office, you seemed to be set on that particular piece of ground. What is it about the old Harkins place that makes you want it so bad? Have you even seen the homestead?"

"Not with my own eyes—I was in such a hurry to file that I didn't make it out here. But I know just what it looks like. You see, I used to be employed by the Harkins family, doing chores and acting as nanny for their daughter, Louise Rose, until they moved west." Emma relaxed her posture. Talking about her heart's home made her just plain wistful inside.

"I used to get letters from Mrs. Harkins. Lands, how she loved her beautiful wood-framed house. It was like a palace compared to her neighbors' dugouts and soddies. She says the yard is full of flowers and a creek runs close by. She planted a hundred trees, which have got to have three or four seasons' growth on them by now.

"There's a well in the yard, and a barn for Pearl. It broke Mrs. Harkins's heart to quit the claim, but Louise Rose was a wild one. To think of the nights I stayed up watching to see that she didn't sneak out her window to take up with some low 'count!

"Anyway, Mrs. Harkins wrote to say they had to move on. No doubt it had to do with Louise Rose, but the prime spot they were leaving behind was free for the taking if I could get here in time to be the first to claim it. So here I am, Mr. Suede, bound for paradise."

"Hell in a basket, ma'am. Hell in a basket." Matt Suede sighed deeply, then didn't say another word for the rest of the trip.

From a quarter mile off, Matt saw the very thing he knew to be true. The Harkins place was no better than any other struggling homestead. Maybe it was worse, having been abandoned. There was no trace of a fine wood house gleaming in the moonlight, no barn, no half-grown trees, no trace of Emma Parker's dream.

Any second now he would have to tell her that they had passed over the boundaries of her land. He'd rather have a steer stomp on his foot than see the high spirits making her strain forward in the seat turn to slump-shouldered sorrow.

How did a man find the words to break a person's dream? Especially the person who had so recently saved his neck from a noose.

"Whoa!" he called to the team. Emma Parker looked up at him with moonlight caught in the glow of her eyes. "We're here, ma'am. This is the old Harkins place."

Emma climbed over the side of the wagon before he had a chance to help her down. She walked about thirty yards, then turned and glanced all about. She hadn't taken the time to change out of her fancy gown before they'd headed out of town, so now, standing out in the moonlight, she looked like an angel who'd lost her wings and was searching high and low for them.

"I think you've brought me to the wrong place, Mr. Suede."

Matt jumped off the wagon. His footfalls crunching over the dirt echoed across the prairie. Somewhere, not too far off, a cow bellowed and another, farther out, answered.

"This is what you filed on. It's the old Harkins place."

"But this can't be it." He'd come up close enough to hear the swallowed sob in her throat. "Where's my house? Where's Pearl's barn?"

"There'll be a dugout around here, most likely. Was your Mrs. Harkins prone to tall tales? Well, even if she wasn't, the house wouldn't have lasted the month. Out here, lumber is like gold. Mrs. Harkins's house is scattered all over the county by now."

"Mercy, I don't even see a single tree." Emma made a full turn, looking far and wide over her land. "Do you suppose my neighbors took them, too?"

How was he to tell her that her nearest neighbor was probably a two-hour ride back to town? Pendragon's crew had taken up so many homesteads circling Dodge that Matt was surprised this one had been overlooked.

A sudden gust of wind snatched Emma's skirt. The satin snapped and twisted. Out over the plains, dust began to stir. Cowboys would be herding their beeves toward the shelter of gullies and shallow hills. In another ten minutes a man wouldn't be able to see his own boots.

"Darlin'." Already Matt had to raise his voice to be heard over the moan of the wind. "Unhitch Thunder and Pearl. Take them over to that rise and see if you can find the dugout. Call out if there's still a door on it."

Matt took the canvas cover off the wagon without looking at it. He kept his gaze on the blur of Emma's gown. For now he could see it, but in a minute or two she could blow all the way back to Dodge and he wouldn't know it.

"I found it!" Luckily her voice blew right at him. "There's no door!"

He hadn't expected a door. "Go inside, yell if there's enough room for the other horses!" He wasn't sure if she heard his voice, but the half-obscured glow of her gown vanished, telling him that she had gone inside.

Matt leaped up on the wagon, praying that his bride was a sensible sort and had brought along a few tools.

"There's room and more, Mr. Suede."

Emma's voice came from the rear wheel of the wagon.

"Hell, ma'am, what are you doing out here? You should have stayed put, where it was safe."

"You don't expect me to stay inside while my goods blow to kingdom come?"

"That's just what I expect." Matt hopped down from the wagon. "Here, take hold of my arm and don't let go."

Matt gripped the team's reins and with the wagon in tow, made slow progress toward the dugout tucked into the hillside.

Praise be that the trip from town hadn't taken a few minutes longer. The last thing he needed was to be caught out in a sandstorm with a defenseless woman who fancied herself capable of living in the wild with a blind horse as her protector.

Emma had taken only a few steps, with her skirts tangling about her shins, before she started to cough. She'd never known a wind that could steal the breath right out of a body. Sand and grit stung her face, forcing her to close her eyes. Thank goodness Mr. Suede had a strong arm to clutch onto.

"Stand still a minute, darlin'." A cloth smelling like dust and hardworking male came across her face. She felt Matt Suede's fingers at the back of her head, tying a knot in it.

She took a deep, sand-free breath, with her new husband leading the way toward the dugout. She couldn't see, but she felt safer beside this big, solid man.

Matt let go of the horses and led her inside. She took the bandanna from her face and shook it out. Even with her eyes uncovered, she couldn't see Pearl or Thunder at the far end of the cavelike home.

With no door on the dugout, the wind whipped inside, swirling and moaning off the walls.

"Mr. Suede, are you in here?" No answer. What could have happened to him? "Mr. Suede?"

"I'll be along." His words came out coughed more than spoken. "Stay inside."

Emma heard the jingling of a harness just beyond the opening to the soddie. She took four dust-blinded steps outside before she ran smack into his vest.

"Hell, woman, I thought I told you to stay inside."

"You'll need this." Emma felt for his face. Her fingers touched his unshaven cheek. She tied the bandanna around it. "And you can't tell me what to do."

Leather snapped, metal jingled and Matt Suede pulled her and the rented team into the dugout.

He yanked the bandanna off his face. If she stared hard, she could make out his features in the dark. He didn't look pleased.

"Didn't you vow before God and Mrs. Sizeloff to obey your husband?"

"You are not my husband, not really."

"Do I have to frame that marriage license and hang it on the wall?"

The wind slapped Matt Suede's shirtsleeves against his arms. It whirled the dirt on the floor, making it dance about his boots.

"Did you bring any tools or lamps in the wagon?"

"Yes, of course. I'm not a half-wit."

He gave her a long stare through the gloom.

"If you tell me where they are I'll tack the canvas over the doorway. We'll be able to light a lamp."

"You won't be able to get to them. They're in the bottom crate toward the front."

He yanked the bandanna over his nose and turned to go out. She caught his arm.

"Please stay inside—we'll get by until the wind lets up."

"It could turn bitter cold."

"I've been cold before. It never lasts."

Emma felt her way to a corner of the room. The wind was quiet here, but he had been right about the cold. The temperature seemed to be dropping by the second. She sat down in the dirt and drew her knees up to her chest.

This ought to finish off her hard-earned gown. She had hoped to sell it after today, but there was no chance for that now. Still, the fabric might be salvaged for curtains when the day came that she had windows to put them in.

She heard Matt settle into the corner across from her. *Thank glory for the darkness.* She couldn't bear it if he saw the way her shoulders shook with cold and disappointment. How would she ever make her dream come true now? Had she saved ever so long to end up in a cave? Oh, the tales she'd spun for herself and Pearl.

She did have land, though. Some of it turned to mud on her face while quiet tears slipped down her cheeks.

Boot steps thumped on the packed floor. Her husband settled down beside her with one lean thigh brushed up beside hers. He tucked the canvas that had covered the wagon over them both and laid his arm around her shoulder.

"I believe that since we're wed, I'll start to call you Emma."

The chill that had made her tremble faded under his hand rubbing briskly up and down her arm.

"Since that's the case, I'll call you Matt."

"Darlin', what made you want to come to this wild place all on your own?" His hand slowed until the rub softened to a caress. The caress tugged her up tight against his chest. "It's a bold thing for a little lady to do."

Warmth flooded her until she felt liquid rather than jittery. "I thought you were going to call me Emma."

"That's exactly what I'm calling you. Emma, darlin', why'd you do it?"

"I needed something of my own." She shrugged her shoulders. It was a simple dream, really, a common one that came true hundreds of times a day for other folks.

"All my life I've been doing for others," she said. "This was going to be my place in the world where I could stay and stay. No one to tell me 'Emma, we no longer need your services. Time to find a new home and a new family.' I vow, I'll never keep another person's home or raise another person's child again."

Emma nodded her head to emphasize the point. She felt the air hitch in Matt's lungs.

"Don't you like younglings?"

"Oh, I like them just fine." Emma enjoyed the brush of Matt's strong shoulder shifting up and down under her cheek with each of his deep, slow breaths. She snuggled in closer to it. "I'm much too fond of them, in fact. About the time I think of them as my own, I'm off to another position. I don't believe my heart could take losing another one."

A horse stomped and snorted. The wind whistled and moaned inside, but it roared like a fury outside.

"Why do you rob banks?"

"Not for any love of thievery. I'm not a natural criminal. Though I do admit that I leaned that way when I was a kid, but I learned quick enough that I wanted to live past fifteen."

He rested his cheek on the top of her head with a sigh that shuddered through his chest. Emma felt every bit of it, being hugged close for the shared warmth.

"I rob banks because of a promise I made to a dying friend."

"Do you believe in keeping promises, no matter what? Like as not, your friend wouldn't want you to hang."

"I keep all my promises, Emma. Especially this one."

Matt started to sing. His mellow crooning soothed her. The curve of her breast lay on top of his muscular forearm. Surely it was common sleepiness making her feel like honey being stirred in hot tea.

For some reason she didn't mind that. She took the lovely sensation right along into a dream.

Chapter Three

Moments before sunrise, Matt opened his eyes. As a cowboy he was accustomed to waking early. He enjoyed night shifts watching over the herd, as well. Trail dust and cowhide were perfume to him.

Spring had been his last roundup, but he had set enough money aside to last for some time. With Hawker getting out of prison, he'd be moving to California and fall roundup would go on without him.

Apparently Emma was an early riser. The horses had been taken out of the dugout. Her gown lay folded in a corner of the sod cube with his hat set on top of it.

Matt stood, smoothed out his clothes and grabbed his hat. Morning light could be bright as the dickens, so he tugged the brim low and went outside. No doubt his bride was waiting for him to hitch up the team for the ride back to town. He felt her sorrow. Dreams had a way of dying hard.

At some point on the long ride back, he'd have to tell her about Lucy and the boys.

He didn't see Emma or the horses, but he noticed

that she'd been going through the boxes in the wagon. A few of them lay open on the ground beside the wheel.

A horse whickered near the creek. He couldn't see it beyond the brush, but he figured Emma must be there, as well.

Near the water, a whiff of coffee teased his nose. The things a mind could conjure way out here. First thing back in town, he'd take Emma for a late breakfast, and then over a cup, he'd break the news about Lucy. That seemed safe enough. In a public place she might not make a scene.

Matt stepped through the shrubbery. He froze with his mouth half-open in greeting.

Emma sat on a wood crate beside the creek wearing only her underclothes.

"Considering everything, Pearl, I believe we'll make out just fine," she said.

She twisted a hank of wet hair in her hands. Water dribbled over her chemise and sucked it to her skin. She might as well have left the frilly thing off for all that it shielded her well-favored curves from his gaze.

She picked up a brush and tugged it through the mass of soaking hair.

Because he was standing stiff as a stick, she didn't notice him at first. When she did, she smiled up through a beam of sunshine.

"Morning, Matt." She set down her brush and pointed to a pot of coffee that she had heating on a small fire beside the crate. "If that marriage license is as genuine as you claim it is, sit here with me and have a cup."

He took the pot and poured a mugful. He sat across from her, but blamed if he could keep his eyes from

darting to the sweet pink nipples poking at the thin
fabric of her chemise.

"Your face is blushing. Don't tell me you're embar-
rassed to see your wife in her shift?" Emma picked up
her own cup of coffee and took a deep swallow. Her
damp throat muscles constricted.

"I've seen a shift or two in the past, but darlin', yours
is soaked right through."

Emma plucked at the fabric. "If it troubles you, you
can turn your back, but with the way the day is heating
up, it'll be dry by the time we finish this pot."

Matt grinned. So far married life didn't seem so bad.

"I've been wondering about that right pretty gown
you had on yesterday. You must have planned it special for some man."

Emma set the brush in her lap and sighed. The drying fabric of her shift tightened over curves that a man
could fill his hands with. "Not so long ago I thought I
could find contentment with a Mr. Fredrick Winn. Just
in time, I realized that all he wanted was a wife to do
for him. He figured he'd get for free what others had
paid me for. Just in time, I got Mrs. Harkins's letter and
knew I had another choice."

Hoofbeats pounded the earth. Matt stood and peered
through the brush. Hell, if it didn't look like the boys
coming on fast, and there was Lucy, her blond curls
bouncing like springs, riding in the saddle in front of
Jesse.

He sure wouldn't be able to explain their existence
to Emma gently now.

"Company's coming," he announced.

"Blast!" Emma jumped up beside him to peer
through the brush. "My first guests and I'm half naked!"

Emma plucked her calico dress from its resting place on a bush and wriggled it over her head. In her haste she had some trouble with the buttons, so he helped, starting with the ones just over her breasts.

"You seem to have some experience with buttons, Matt."

Just when the last little button slipped into place the visitors reined in before the dugout. Matt took his wife by the elbow and led her out into the open.

With Jesse's help, Lucy slid off the horse.

"Papa!" She ran to him as fast as her four-year-old legs could go. "Papa!"

Matt squatted low and opened his arms to the little girl. He scooped her up and swung her in a circle. Emma's mind reeled.

The girl had called Matt *Papa*...twice. Her small hands hugged his neck while she smacked kisses all over his beard-shadowed face.

What had she gotten herself into?

The three men who had ridden in with the little girl dismounted their horses, grinning as wide as faces would allow.

"Good to see you again, ma'am." This was the red-headed boy from the land office. He took off his hat and covered his heart with it. "I'm Red, Texas Red."

"Mrs. Suede." A man about Matt's age with a heavy black mustache and curly hair to match extended his gloved hand in greeting. Warm leather folded over Emma's fingers. "Name's Cousin Billy."

"Pleased to meet you," Emma murmured to be polite, but "astounded" would be a more honest thing to say.

Who were these men and why did they feel a need to

show up at her doorstep, or what would be her doorstep, an hour after sunup? Surely it didn't take three men to deliver one little girl.

"Congratulations, ma'am." Emma recognized the third man, grinning and slapping his thigh with his hat, as Jesse, the owner of the livery in Dodge.

"Papa." The little girl's voice grew suddenly shy. She tucked her blond curly head under Matt's chin and peered at Emma with shining blue eyes. "Is that my new ma?"

Matt's mouth tugged down at the corners. He looked tense.

"Lucy, baby, we talked about your ma, remember?" He rocked her while he spoke in a voice so soothing it made Emma wonder what it would be like to be held up in those big strong arms, safe from all the troubles going on down below.

Lucy nodded her head.

"Your mama loved you so much. I recall how she held you close and kissed your little bald head on the day you were born. The last thing she said before the angels came to take her was that we should call you Lucy." Lucy stuck her thumb in her mouth and began to suck. While Matt spoke, she gazed at Emma with wide eyes, her expression a mixture of hope and doubt. "Your mama sees you every day from heaven."

Lucy glanced up at her father. She plucked her thumb from her mouth.

"But I don't see her. I want a mama that I can see. I want that lady to be my mama."

"Darlin', you can't just pick out a ma like you pick out candy in the mercantile."

"Silly Papa, I know that. Red said since you married that lady, she's my ma."

"For now, let's just call her Emma."

Lucy frowned, then wiggled down out of her father's arms. She looked up at Emma.

"Mama, can I go to the creek and look for frogs?"

"Don't go into the water and stay away from the horses," she said without thinking. How many times had she given such an answer to a child? "And stay out in the open where we can see you."

"You'd make a fine mother if you had a mind to do it." Matt had stepped close, whispering while she watched Lucy skip toward the creek.

"Well, I don't have a mind to." She grabbed her drying hair and twisted it in a bun at her neck. "I've done all the raising of children that I intend to do."

"Excuse me, Mrs. Suede." Cousin Billy's boots crunched across the dirt. He stood before her twisting his hat in his leather gloves. Red and Jesse peeked out from behind his tall, broad back. "The boys and I wonder if we've come too late and missed breakfast."

"Breakfast!" Why, her life hadn't changed a bit! Now it was worse. Strangers wanted to be fed instead of employers.

"Whoa there, boys." Only a blind man would miss the red-hot temper flaring in her cheeks. Matt grimaced. "Take a look around and tell me where you'd expect my wife to fix you a meal. There's nothing here but a flea-bitten dugout."

Matt stepped between her and the three offended-looking men, and just in time. If they'd stood there a second longer, gaping at her as though she'd betrayed

her womanly calling, she'd have done something re-
grettable.

With an arm slung about Red's shoulders Matt
pointed the half-famished trio toward the creek.

"Just because Emma married me doesn't oblige her
to keep your bellies filled. There's coffee down by the
creek. After you've had your fill, get the horses hitched
up for the trip back to town."

Relief kicked the breath back into her lungs. Her
heart slid out of her throat and back into her bosom.
For one heart-fluttering moment she had feared that
these men intended to stay. As soon as they unloaded
the goods remaining in her wagon, it would be just
Emma and Pearl.

Down by the creek Emma heard Lucy's laughter.
Red hopped about in the water, apparently hot on the
trail of the little girl's frog.

"He's a fat one!" Emma heard Red call out.

She watched Lucy hop up and down, clapping her
hands in delight. If the men hadn't eaten before they
rode out this morning, odds were that they hadn't
thought to feed Lucy, either.

She could certainly spare a can of peaches and some
crackers for the child. A bite or two for Texas Red
wouldn't be out of line, since he wasn't yet fully a man.

The others didn't deserve anything, since grown men
should have thought to tend to their own needs. All except Matt, who hadn't had time for even a bite since
they'd left Dodge last night.

"Oh, drat!" If she was going to feed some, she had
to feed all. This hungry gang would use up a fair portion of her supplies. She'd have to go back to town to

make up for it, but she needed a new front door before nightfall, anyway.

"Matt!" Emma picked up the hem of her skirt and hurried after him as he strode toward the creek. "Tell your friends I'll cook them breakfast, but just this once."

The breakfast that Emma had rustled up was as good as Matt had ever tasted, but it hit his stomach uneasily.

From a quarter mile across the blowing grass, he watched Emma astride her blind horse. She rode about gazing at land that looked pretty much the same one direction as another.

She would be saying goodbye to it and the dream that had brought her so many miles from home. Matt knew about giving up land that lay so deep in the soul that the tramp of the beeves' hooves upon the soil felt like a heartbeat.

"Papa, can I keep Mr. Hoppety?"

Matt snapped his gaze back to his circle of family seated on the ground, absorbed in Emma's fine vittles. He swallowed his melancholy and smiled at his daughter.

"Mr. Hoppety wouldn't take to town living. Frogs need to be near the creek."

Lucy climbed onto his lap and opened her palms, revealing the frog. "But I'd take some creek water along."

"Some things can't take to a new home, darlin'. Hoppety would be one of them." He thought of his mother—she had been another. "You take him on back to the creek, now. We've got to load things up and get back to town."

"I'll come and visit you some day," Lucy crooned

into the frog's ear. She sighed, deep and resigned, but turned and with slow steps walked toward the creek.

"Speaking of keeping things," Billy said, wiping a crumb from his mustache, "what are you going to do with a wife?"

Last night in the dark he'd had an idea of what to do with her, but now, in the practical light of day, he wasn't so sure.

He'd made a vow to protect her, but a nagging voice deep in his gut warned him that his bride didn't want protecting.

"For now, I'm going to take her back to town." Matt stood. He watched Emma riding back with a sunny smile on her face. Maybe she had a better idea of where they were going than he did. "Let's load up that wagon and head on back to Dodge, boys."

Emma's pretty face lifted his spirits enough to let him sing while he walked down to the stream to get the rented team.

Lucy plopped the frog into the water. Her lower lip trembled when she glanced up, so Matt made his song a funny one about Mr. Hoppety being crowned king of the creek.

"Mr. Hoppety thinks you sing silly, Papa," she said, but her lips stopped quivering and turned into a laugh.

Matt glanced up when he heard hoofbeats splashing across the creek. For a blind horse, Pearl trotted forward with amazing confidence. She didn't see him or Lucy as she cantered up the bank of the stream, but Emma did.

The lovely smile that had reached him over the waving grass had turned into a frown that made poor Mr. Hoppety squeeze under a rock.

"Lucy, there's a tin of cookies in the wagon. Ask Red

to get one for you," Emma said, her lips looking as tight as a string on a fiddle.

"Red!" Lucy called, half running, half skipping toward the wagon. "Mama said to find me a cookie!"

Whatever had gotten under Emma's bustle must be something he wanted to keep clear of if she didn't want to discuss it in front of Lucy.

"Guess I'll get a cookie, too." Matt hurried after his daughter, hoping to be halfway to the wagon before Emma had a chance to speak so that he could pretend he didn't hear her.

"Unload my wagon while you're doing it." For a small woman, her voice carried like a trail boss's.

It was hard to pretend not to hear insanity. Matt stopped and pivoted on his boot heel. He studied her face, praying that the determination settling in didn't really mean that she intended to stay here.

"We're going back to town, darlin'. Unloading that wagon would be purely foolish."

"The five of you are free as can be to take the wagon and go back to town, but my goods are staying here with me."

What had ever made him think this woman favored a delicate flower? She might be tiny, her skin might resemble petals and her scent nectar, but her roots were stubborn as weeds.

Apparently, once she had her mind set on a course, it was roped and tied. He'd have to do some mighty fine convincing to show her how wrong she was.

Matt pressed two fingers to his lips and let out a shrill whistle. Thunder, faithful as the best of dogs, trotted up from the creek shaking his full glossy mane. If only women could be more like horses.

He leaped up on Thunder's back, bringing him close to Emma and Pearl.

"I believe we need to ride a bit, Mrs. Suede. We have a few matters to work through."

"I believe we do, Mr. Suede."

Emma urged her horse to take the lead, but Pearl, being a proper female, seemed happy to trail along after Thunder.

They had ridden well away from the dugout and still Matt hadn't spoken a single word. Hopefully, he wouldn't. It would be ever so easy if he kept quiet while she convinced him that he and his child should return to town while she remained here.

"I'm sure, since you have nothing to say, you've come to see that the only fitting thing is for you and Lucy to go home to Dodge. You can tell the marshal that I turned out to be as foul tempered as the number two-rooster in the barnyard." Since she was not well acquainted with the man, he couldn't say otherwise.

"I could tell him that."

Was that a grin playing at the corners of his mouth? "You could tell him that Lucy didn't take to me."

"Now, that would be a lie."

"If you're going to tell one, you might as well tell two."

Matt barked out a laugh.

"I'm not much for lying." He reined Thunder to a stop, then leaned forward in the saddle with his elbow resting on the horn. "And I do keep my vows."

"You can rob all the banks you've a mind to, if it will keep your friend happy, but go away and leave me in peace."

All of a sudden it felt as if bees buzzed inside her. She didn't want to say anything cruel to him—after all, he'd made her dream come true, or what there was of it. She swung off the saddle. A good stroll over her land should calm her down.

Imagine him believing that she had the temper of a second rooster! She'd taken only two steps when she heard the click of a gun's hammer.

"Get back in the saddle…now." His voice had become as hard as the metal he gripped in his fist. "Don't argue, just do it."

She took another step away from Pearl. "Why you low-down w—"

The mouth of the gun flashed orange. A puff of earth exploded near her foot. The blast sent Pearl on a run back over the creek.

Emma felt a scream gathering in her throat, but she turned it into a foul word.

"Rattlers sometimes travel in pairs." He scooted back in the saddle as far as he could. "If I were you I'd climb up here on Thunder."

She glanced down. Lordy! Only the fact that Matt had shot the viper's head off had kept her from stepping on it. It took only a second for her to reach Thunder's side and lift a trembling hand to Matt. He pulled her up into the saddle ahead of him, then turned the horse to follow the river, south, away from the homestead.

"Darlin', you just might be the death of me. Let me have a look at your shoes."

Since he seemed so determined that they were truly married, she yanked her skirt nearly to her knee. She turned the shoe, one half of her prettiest pair, this way and that.

"Any woman who goes homesteading in dancing slippers needs to be watched out for."

The nerve of him, pointing out the error of her footwear! She'd put them on only because she had been thinking of the way she and Matt had fit together so easily under that canvas last night.

"What kind of a man brings a little girl to a place where snakes look the same as the dirt?"

"Lucy just turned four years old, but she's known how to keep clear of snakes since she hit the ground walking."

Holding on to a temper against someone who had just saved her life proved purely difficult.

"I don't know why it is, Matt, but every now and then you bring out the pickle in me." Why was that? Most of her life she'd been the soul of kindness to nearly everyone she'd met. "Well, once again I'm sorry I called you that name."

"Wasn't such a bad name, considering I'd just fired a gun at your feet for no good reason that you knew of." His words rustled the top of her hair when he spoke. The hard, shifting muscles of his chest grazed her back with each clip-clop of Thunder's hooves.

If she let herself believe that they were truly wed, there would be some things about marriage that she would like to explore. Things to do with the fact that Matt's abdomen was no longer flat where her backside rocked against him to the sway of the horse's stride.

In the past, she'd tried not to wonder about such things. When they popped into her mind she dismissed them by focusing her thoughts on some task that needed doing. It didn't take long to learn that curiosity had a will of its own.

Now that she was a married woman, it might not hurt to let her imagination dwell on Matt's anatomy. Especially that part that had suddenly sprung to life behind her.

The problem with letting her mind roam free was that it did some troubling things to her body. She had to wiggle in the saddle to ease the strange twisting in her belly.

All at once Matt slipped off Thunder's back to walk alongside the horse. He'd turned quiet again, but it was easy to see that thoughts ran wild in his mind. Maybe the stirrings going on between them reminded him of Lucy's mother.

It shouldn't trouble Emma to be the second wife. Indeed, yesterday afternoon she'd have been happy to be anyone's tenth.

"Matt...what was your first wife like?"

"You'd be the one to know that, darlin'." He glanced up at her with his hat shading his face. She'd been a fool to leave her bonnet behind with the sun beating down, even as early as it was. "Until you came upon me in the livery, I'd never given matrimony more than a passing thought."

Matt led Thunder to the creek and let his reins fall free. He gave Emma a hand down from the horse.

"Let's sit here for a spell. There are some things you need to know about the boys and me."

Emma sat down beside the water. This July morning was a blister. She took off her shoes, rolled off her stockings, then hiked up her skirt to her knees. If this talk was leading to her sharing her homestead, she'd need cool water on her feet to put out her temper. It would be a humiliation to have to apologize a third time for calling her husband an ugly name.

"The water's as cool as can be." Emma scooped up a handful and let it run over her face and down her neck. "Take off those boots and see."

He followed her example, even to the scoop of water, then he took off his hat and put it on her head. He might have scolded her about forgetting something so important, but he only tugged the brim down so that her eyes were shaded against the glare of the sun on the water.

"When I was a kid, Emma, I was as wild as they come. Wasn't a soul in town would bet a quarter that I'd grow to be a man. Just in time, I found out life was a fine thing and I wanted to live as much of it as I could.

"During those years I had a friend. No...he was more like a brother. Utah's the one who made me give a lick for myself. He convinced me to put away my quick guns and take up with him on the roundups. Jesse, Utah, Cousin Billy and I all signed up to cowboy Pendragon's herds, and some others around Dodge.

"It was a fine life, the four of us so young and full of adventure. One day, Utah went sweet on a gal from town. I think all of us went sweet on her. But Utah's the one who married her. She died the next year giving birth to Lucy. After a time, Mrs. Conner over at the boardinghouse minded Lucy while Utah went back to herding cows with Billy, Jesse and me.

"It wasn't like old times, though. We'd all grown up over the pain. Then it wasn't six months later that we lost Utah, too."

Tears itched at the back of Emma's eyes. Matt's face looked full of sorrow, as if he had gone back to those days and the old pain had turned fresh again.

"We were rounding up one afternoon. Utah was on the far side of the herd from the rest of us. He was talking to little Lenore, Pendragon's twelve-year-old daughter. He thought she'd be more comfortable with a blanket under her saddle. That's how Utah was, always looking out for others. Well, he tied that red blanket, but it came loose sometime later and was dragging on the ground behind her. For some reason, that spooked the cattle and they started running. Little Lenore saw what was happening and reached around to tie the blanket behind her. She lost her balance and fell off with the cows coming right at her. We couldn't get across to her, but Utah was already on that side of the herd.

"He called out for her to stay still. He got to her in time, but the cinch on his saddle gave under the weight of lifting her. Lenore's horse, not being properly trained for cattle work, had run off. By then Utah's horse was too skittish to recall his training and took off after the other horse. That left the pair of them standing in the way of the panicked herd with no way to escape.

"Billy and I were halfway through the herd when Utah picked up the blanket and headed off across the prairie. Somehow he managed to turn the stampede away from Lenore. He saved her life, but there was nothing left for Utah but to turn and face the cattle. His six-gun rang out. We all heard five shots. The leading steer went down and the one after, but we couldn't get to Utah until it was too late."

Emma wanted to say how sorry she was, but mere words seemed so pitiful. She reached out and covered his hand where he fingered little circles in the water sliding by. He glanced sideways and seemed surprised, but he slipped his calloused fingers through hers and squeezed them.

"The three of us made it over to him before he passed. He asked me to take Lucy as my own and bring her up right. I made a vow as though I was doing something for Utah, but the truth is that raising his little girl became a blessing.

"It's for Lucy that The Ghost robs the bank. Pendragon never felt responsible for providing for her, even though Utah died to rescue his own Lenore. If there's one thing that man values, it's a dollar."

Emma remembered the careless dropping of ashes on the sidewalk and how they had dirtied the hem of her dress. The smug set of his face when he had stepped out of the land office had confirmed that he had high regard for his own position. Apparently no one else mattered. Her original dislike of him was now confirmed.

"As I see it, Matt, The Ghost is only taking what is Lucy's due without a bit of crime involved." What a relief to know that she hadn't hitched up with a villain. "I'm proud to know The Ghost."

"If that's the case, there are four of us to be proud to know. My cousin, Billy, sets things up with the costume and such, and Jesse provides a horse then hides it while I get out of my disguise. Young Red does his part well away from the actual crime. He keeps the rumors flying about The Ghost."

And a very good job he did. Emma couldn't help a quiet laugh when she remembered Red's sincerity while he told her to watch for The Ghost.

"I'll keep your secret." Emma laughed again and splashed up some water with her toes.

All of a sudden Matt grabbed her by the shoulders

and pressed her back against the bank. He rolled on top of her and kissed her. The world seemed to drift away while his mouth moved over hers, just the way it had done during their wedding vows.

Nothing existed but the nuzzle of Matt's lips, firm and prickly on top, since he needed a shave. The world narrowed to the scent of his skin. The weight of his body, sprawled on top of her, twisted and tickled her belly way down low. She wished he would touch her in places she had never been touched. Was it a sin to become one flesh in a marriage that would last only a day?

"Darlin'." Matt lifted his head enough to gaze down at her. "I told you before, I keep my vows. Those we took before Mrs. Sizeloff were as binding as any I've ever made."

Emma figured he was probably lying on top of her so she wouldn't have the air to speak, but somehow she didn't mind that, just now.

"You are my wife in every way I ever heard of but one. Now, I'd like to make you come back to town with me…hold on, before you call me a mean name, just hear me out. Coming back to town would be the sensible thing, but I know you're set on putting down roots out here."

His brown eyes warmed to amber. Lordy, if she wasn't about to melt away into the creek!

"Would you be willing to stay married to me until summer's end? We'd live here with Lucy, Red and Billy instead of in town. That way, I'd be safe from the marshal and you won't be out here alone. Before autumn we'll ride on out of your life like we were never there."

"Why would I want to take on the care of grown men?"

"Because you wouldn't last the week out here by yourself. Like as not, you'll be snakebit by nightfall. As for the grown men, cattle aren't all we know. We'll build you a house, Emma, and a barn for Pearl."

Emma bit her bottom lip trying to ground herself. A woman could forget to breathe if she gazed into those golden-amber eyes long enough.

"A proper house out of wood?"

"I took a vow to keep and protect you. That house will see to it once I've gone."

A woman never did know when a venomous snake might slither into sight, and Matt did offer a fair trade.

"I believe you've got yourself a bargain. Now let me up before summer's over and nothing gets done."

And before she could dwell on the sudden hitch in her heart. The man was a temptation she would struggle with. The last thing she wanted was to finally have a home of her own, only to pine away for the man who had built it.

Chapter Four

From a block away Matt heard the crack of a hammer slamming against wood. The echo seemed to wrap around his neck and knot the breath in his throat.

He'd purposely taken the long way to the dry goods store so that Emma and Lucy wouldn't see the gallows that had been erected overnight. He'd seen this kind of thing happen often enough to know that the distant hammering was a coffin being built. Some poor soul was gazing through the jail bars, looking at his last afternoon.

If it hadn't been for Emma's quick thinking yesterday, there might have been a double hanging. Matt's employer would have purchased his own justice as quick as a lick.

Pendragon figured that in Dodge, money powered the gavel, and he knew how to spend his cash.

Just when he was about to usher Emma and Lucy into the general store, the marshal stepped out of the Long Branch one door up. He gave Matt a sizing up that made him wonder if he'd shouted those thoughts about getting hanged.

"'Rath and Wright, Dealers in Everything.'" Emma read the sign over the door, then snapped her parasol closed. "Do you suppose they have something cheerful to cover the dugout walls?"

"They have candy." Lucy tugged on Emma's skirt and looked up at her with hopeful eyes. "Can I have some? Please, Mama?"

The marshal seemed too interested in what went on between the three of them. If Emma declared that she wasn't Lucy's mother, he might get more suspicious than he already was.

Emma glanced at Lucy and opened her mouth to say something, but she must have caught sight of the lawman, because she pinched her mouth closed.

She patted Lucy's head and smiled lovingly at her.

"You go on along inside and pick out what you want. Papa and I will be along shortly."

"Sugar lump," Emma said with a sigh as soon as Lucy was out of sight. She swaggered up to Matt, so close that her calico-clad bosom brushed his buckskin vest. She stood up on her toes. Her fingertips traced curly hearts on his shirtsleeve. She whispered in his ear, but the secret was loud enough for the marshal to overhear.

"You know how long I've dreamed of being mama to that little girl, but I'll purely die if we can't sneak away by ourselves for the rest of the afternoon."

Emma's teeth nipped his earlobe. Heat flashed up and down his body. He turned his face. The long kiss that he sipped from her lips felt too hot to have been for the marshal's benefit alone.

She knocked back his hat and feathered his hair through her fingers from scalp to collar, all the while keeping up with his kiss. She didn't take a breath until he heard the marshal's boots stomp down the boardwalk.

At last she let loose of him, sliding down until her boot heels clicked on the sidewalk. Her lashes lay like sable against her pink cheeks. Her chest heaved as if she had just danced the length of Front Street.

All at once she shook herself and opened her eyes. She spun about and followed the path that Lucy had taken.

"Surely there's something inside to cover up that dirt on the dugout floor."

The hell with the dugout floor! How could she be thinking of coverings after the moment they'd just shared?

It might have begun for the benefit of the marshal, but that's not how it had ended. He could hardly walk a straight line into Rath and Wright's with all the goings-on beneath his jeans.

By the time Matt's eyes adjusted to the dim interior of the store, his insides had settled enough to focus on the reason they had come to town. Shopping was no more than a chore to him, but Emma and Lucy looked happy as butterflies in a meadow.

For a woman who spurned mothering, Emma appeared to take right to it. She kept hold of Lucy's plump hand while she pointed out this and that object of purchase.

Lucy wanted ribbon for her hair. Emma pulled three colors from the shelf. She knelt on the floor, eye to eye with the child.

"I think pink is your color." Emma dangled a length

of pink beside Lucy's face. "Which one do you like on me Lucy, yellow or blue?"

His little girl sparkled. She had been asking for a mother since she'd learned to talk. There were some things that a pa couldn't do as well as a ma. He was of no use at all picking out frilly notions.

His heart took a warm turn but came up short when he thought about California. Lucy would become attached to Emma over the summer. The inevitable separation might break her heart.

"It's only been a day, but already the three of you look like a family. More the glory to God."

Matt hadn't noticed Mrs. Sizeloff come into the store. He'd been so involved in watching the ribbon picking that the world had gone on without his notice.

"Thank you, ma'am." Matt took off his hat and twisted it in his hand. Mrs. Sizeloff cradled a newborn in the crook of her arm while her son, Charlie, tugged on her skirt urging her toward the counter displaying hard candies.

"I was telling my Josie just last night that you and Mrs. Suede looked near as happy as we did on our wedding day. Oh, my, weren't those happy times?" The preacher looked dreamy for a moment, then seemed to notice the tugging on her skirt. "You'll call on me when it's time for a christening, won't you?"

"Yes, ma'am." How big of a sin was it to lie to a preacher? He needed to remember that Emma's display of affection for him was no more than a show. Even if it weren't, that christening would never happen. He and his wife were traveling the same trail only until fall.

Mrs. Sizeloff followed Charlie to the candy counter and listened to him recite the many sweets that he wanted to take home.

Emma and Lucy had finished with ribbons and moved on to the bolts of fabric stacked near the window. After some discussion, Emma picked out a bolt. She carried it to the counter with Lucy trailing behind, toting a pair of ribbons and a smile.

Mr. Wright took the bolt from Emma's arms and set it on the counter. She greeted Mrs. Sizeloff, then handed her list to the store owner. He looked it over two or three times.

"I've got most of the things you need. Let me just tally up the price for your husband." He put on a pair of spectacles and reached for a pencil.

Matt approached the counter. He wasn't concerned about the cost. He owed Emma more than a house, and he'd been able to put a fair amount away working the roundups. He could take care of Emma without touching what he had put away for Lucy.

"Before you add that up," Emma said, "I wonder if we might do a little bartering, Mr. Wright?"

What was she up to now? Matt took a step back, curious to see what this sweet as a flower, clever as a whip woman was up to.

"What did you have in mind?" Mr. Wright slid his glasses down his nose and set the pencil on the counter.

"Dr. Coonley's Patent Medicine. I have a full case of it. I'll give you a bottle for every two dollars you take off that bill."

She wanted to trade snake oil for durable goods? Who was this woman he had married? She looked like nothing less than an angel, standing there holding Lucy's hand, smiling like sunshine and all the while selling sin in a bottle.

"No offense intended, but folks can get all the spirits they want next door at the Long Branch," Mr. Wright said.

Emma gasped and pressed her fluttering hand against her breast.

"Mr. Wright! I'm offering you pure Orange Lilly. Why, there's not a single harmful ingredient in it. Lands, I take it myself on a monthly basis." Emma leaned across the counter and did that whisper of hers that carried far and wide. "Orange Lilly is for female complaints."

"I'll give you two dollars for it," Mrs. Sizeloff said. "I've been feeling out of sorts since little Maudie was born."

"I've seen that happen to some of the ladies I've worked for over the years. Why, they'd cry and take on for no reason at all after a birthing." Emma touched Mrs. Sizeloff's elbow where it cradled little Maudie. "We're staying at Mrs. Conner's boardinghouse tonight and we'll be here a good part of the day tomorrow. I'll bring a bottle by the church if you'll be there."

"Bless you, Mrs. Suede, that would be kind."

"It's not kind, really. It's business. Orange Lilly will have you feeling better in no time and then you'll tell your friends."

If Emma won over Mrs. Sizeloff, the ladies in town would wear a trail to the homestead looking for healing in a bottle.

He paid Mr. Wright for the goods, then escorted Emma and Lucy out into the afternoon sunshine. It beat down on the sidewalk like a son of a gun.

"You just sold snake oil to the preacher, darlin'." He touched a golden curl that looped alongside her cheek and drew it around his finger. She had the look of a petal blowing in the wind, but apparently she was as wily as any cowboy in Dodge. "You're some kind of a woman."

Emma stared after Matt while he strode toward E. C. Zimmerman's to order the lumber and other supplies they would need to begin building her house. Had she been insulted or praised?

It was hard to tell by the question in his gaze while he stood in front of the mercantile touching her hair as if it was something special. A grin—or a smirk—had flashed across his mouth, but his eyes had sparked with admiration. If she wasn't mistaken, silent laughter cramped his lungs.

Imagine calling pure Orange Lilly snake oil! Why, in a week or so ladies all over town would be free of the female humors plaguing them. At two dollars per humor, well, she'd just see what Matt Suede would call it then.

"Come along, Lucy. There's nothing sweeter for ladies young and old than an afternoon respite."

Hopefully the child would take a nap. That would give Emma an hour or so before dinner to review the list of supplies she'd need to provide for the extra people she would be caring for.

Lucy slipped her hand into Emma's. Having just turned four years old, she still had plump baby fingers. That was one of the things Emma liked about four-year-olds. While they'd grown out of needing constant attention, the blush of babyhood still lingered about them.

The boardinghouse was still three blocks away when Lucy's steps began to drag.

"I'm tired." She rubbed one curled fist over her eye and yawned. A sticky smear of peppermint stick glittered on her lips and fingertips. "Would you carry me, Mama?"

Emma stooped and picked her up. She settled her on her hip. She'd done this so many times with other children that she was sure the curve of her hip had become a chair.

Lucy snuggled her head on Emma's shoulder. The scent of sugar and peppermint made her anxious for the nice dinner at Del Monico's that Matt had promised.

"Lucy, I think you're one of the nicest little girls I've ever met, but I'm not really your mama. You and your papa will be moving back to town when summer's over and I think you should remember that I'm only Emma."

The rhythmic sucking on the peppermint stick slowed, then stopped altogether. A sticky hand dropped from Emma's neck to her waist.

Emma took the candy from the relaxing fist. She held it in the same grip as the parasol and adjusted the angle so that the shade covered the sleeping child.

"I suppose that's a talk we'll have later." Unless she could get Matt to do it.

When she turned off Front Street to make her way up the hill to Mrs. Conner's place, a shadow fell across the boardwalk. Cigarette smoke snaked through the air an instant before a man stepped out in front of her.

Emma tried to walk around him, but he countered and blocked her way.

"Madame." The greeting blew out of the man's mouth along with a whirl of smoke. "Might I congratulate you on your marriage?"

He might, but she'd rather he didn't. Any dot of respect she might have held for Lawrence Pendragon had died when she'd learned of his indifference to Lucy.

"Thank you."

Once again she tried to step around him, but he flicked his smoldering cigarette in her path, then stuck out a shiny black shoe to grind it out.

"The word about town is that you've turned a pair of my best cowboys into homesteaders."

Emma shifted Lucy's weight on her hip and wished that she'd dropped the candy a block back. A woman's full sway was diminished by peppermint dripping down her wrist. "I'd be obliged if you'd let me pass, Mr. Pendragon."

"I'm delighted that you know my name." That blamed shiny shoe continued to take up the sidewalk. Sunlight spit bullets of glare off it as if it was some kind of weapon. "We didn't properly meet outside the land office yesterday."

That's because he'd paid her no more mind than a fly buzzing in the shade. Did he even know that the child asleep on her hip was the baby of the man who had saved his own daughter's life?

"This little girl is getting mighty heavy. Would you mind stepping aside?"

"I beg your pardon." The shoe ground once more at the cigarette but didn't move a hen's feather out of the way. "I have some business I'd like to discuss with you. Here, let me take the little angel while we talk."

"I can't imagine what business a fine gent like you would have with a simple homesteader."

Emma lowered her parasol, shielding Lucy from his outstretched arms. The wonderful thing about a parasol wasn't the shade it provided, but the wicked point on the end. If those long, manicured fingers moved an inch closer to Lucy, he'd find that out.

What kind of a man had smooth pale fingers with long gleaming fingernails, anyway? Mr. Pendragon should pay so much attention to his teeth. Behind the condescending smile he bestowed on her they were as yellow as butter...greasy butter.

"It's the homestead I'd like to discuss with you."

"There's not much to it at the moment." That sallow-toothed worm had land enough of his own. He didn't need to give hers another thought. "I'm sure it's not worth a discussion."

"I'm in control of most of the land out your way. There's not an acre of ground that my cattle don't graze over. I had intended to have one of my men file on that land you took. In another week it would have been part of my spread."

Lawrence Pendragon reached into his vest pocket and took out a small case that reflected enough sunlight to burn Emma's eyes. He took a cigarette out of it, lit it and snapped the case closed.

He took a deep draw, then let out his breath with a curly white hiss.

"Pass the word on to your husband that I'd like to make a fair offer for his place."

"My land isn't for sale." Emma took a half step forward hoping to dislodge the shoe. "Good day, Mr. Pendragon."

"Why, yes, it is a lovely day." A warm breeze snatched his trail of smoke and blew it into the street, cooling the sweat gathering under her hair at the same time. "You should enjoy this day while you can. You may not have many more like it."

Emma gripped the parasol so tightly that her fingers tingled. She bristled at the threat beneath the cultured tones of the man's voice. A fine accent couldn't hide everything.

"And why is that?"

"It's simply the nature of prairie life. One never knows from day to day what might happen. I've seen storms come up in the night that carry homes right away with them. There's drought, there's cattle roaming at will, often over hard-won crops." He lowered his voice. The fingers of one hand twitched against his vest while he stared at the glowing tip of his cigarette. "Anything can cause a prairie fire. A bolt of lightning…or even a careless smoker. So many of my cowboys smoke."

"Are you threatening me, Mr. Pendragon?"

He twisted the end of his mustache and pursed his lips. "I'm simply pointing out the danger that homesteaders face. Wouldn't it be better to accept a generous sum of money in exchange for that dried-out piece of earth, little lady?"

"That's *my* dried-out piece of earth, and I'm not selling it to anyone!" She'd had all she could take of the glittering shoe, so she made a stab at it with the tip of her parasol. Mr. Pendragon took a startled jump backward. Emma hurried past him, but couldn't resist one backward glance.

"And that's Mrs. Matthew Suede to you."

"For the moment." That slowed Emma down. How would he know that? She kept walking, only pretending not to hear if he had something else to say.

"Once Angus Hawker is free, your man is better than dead. You and the little girl will be all alone out there."

* * *

Mrs. Conner's boardinghouse sat atop the rise of a low hill. The front porch overlooked the ruckus going on in town this late July night. Emma sat on a rocker in the dark listening to an argument between a pair of cowboys. Their curses and threats drifted up with the breeze. Farther down the street, rowdy laughter drowned out the bawdy tune being hammered out on a piano.

Emma had no business wondering what her husband of one day was up to, but she did it, anyway. Was he keeping time with a woman he had known before she'd trapped him in the livery, or was he perhaps at the saloon gambling and drinking and listening to the tawdry music?

He could be doing anything. All she really knew of him was that he robbed banks, lived by his word and kissed a woman to steal the heart right out of her bosom.

A shot rang out on Front Street. Four more popped like a string of firecrackers. Cowboy hoots and hollers made Emma long for the quiet of the prairie.

Lucy slept deeply and soundly in one of the two rooms that Matt had rented from Mrs. Conner. Emma had watched her sleep for a while before coming downstairs. The child sucked her thumb and curled her fingers about a bit of satin on her nightgown, apparently oblivious to noise outside.

If it hadn't been for her meeting with Pendragon earlier in the afternoon, Emma would have crawled into bed beside Lucy and closed her ears to the noise as best she could. But anxiety over his comment about a man named Hawker had left her uneasy. In the end, she'd turned down the lamp and left Lucy to sleep in a beam of moonlight shining through the window and onto the bed.

Boots crunched the dirt, beginning the climb up the hill.

"You ain't my pa." Emma recognized Red's voice.

"I'm the closest thing you've got to it, and I say you've got a few more years before you're ready for the Long Branch."

"I'm close on a man. I've got a job and I'm near as tall as you."

"Sweeping up at the land office is a pastime. You get on up to your room and I'll let you know when you're old enough to spend time in the saloon."

"Evening, Emma," Red mumbled in passing. Even with the front door closed behind him, his footsteps sounded heavy on the stairs.

"The boy doesn't know how much growing up he's got between here and manhood." Matt sat in the rocker beside her and stretched out his long legs with his boots crossed at the ankles. "What are you doing out here in the dark, darlin'? It must be close to midnight."

"Half past." Emma watched Matt through the darkness. He took off his hat and shook his hair free of the constraint.

Moonlight shadowed the weary-looking lines at the corners of his mouth and eyes. Her husband was a stranger to her. There was so much she wanted to know about him.

"How many children have you adopted, Matt?" From the way things were going, half the town might start to call her Ma.

"Red's not so much adopted as taken in hand. He came to Dodge about three years ago, ready to face off with the first gunslinger he came across." Matt sat straighter in his chair and propped his elbows on his knees. He gazed down at his hands dangling between his thighs as though the story he was about to tell lay hidden in his fists. "He was almost as wild as I was at his age. Out here in Dodge, when a boy gets off to a bad start, it usually ends in an early grave.

"The first time I saw Red he was about thirty seconds from getting a hole blown in him."

"That's frightful! What happened?"

"I did what needed doing." Matt looked up from his balled-up fists. Midnight shadows couldn't hide the regret in his eyes. "Look, Emma, since we're going to be joining our lives for the rest of the summer, there's some things I expect you have a right to know."

Silence stretched long and thin while he looked out over the nightlife in Dodge, then back at her.

"Sometime or another you'll hear someone call me Singing Trigger Suede. That's because I used to sing while I practiced my quick draw. When I was a kid, I was wild and full of fire and my gun was faster than anything people had seen before. When I was fourteen a man heard about my gun and came to town looking for a fight.

"We faced each other, right down there on that street." Matt grew quiet for a moment, as though he could see it happening again down the hill in the dark. "I was singing through my sweat and my shaking knees, but I knew I could take him. All of a sudden the man turned his back on me and said that he didn't shoot babies. I'd be dead now if he hadn't walked off. It wasn't but an hour later that the man faced someone else at the very same spot. I watched the life blink out of his eyes while he lay there bleeding.

"I put away my gun that afternoon and took to cattle herding. It took some time, but most folks forgot about how fast I could shoot a gun."

"But they still call you Singing Trigger Suede?"

"Some do, the ones who have lived here for a long time. But most folks are newcomers and don't know about my past."

"What about your folks?"

"I hardly remember my pa. He was killed in an accident on our ranch when I was six. My ma tried to make a go of it, but she never took to the hard life out here, even when my pa was alive. When I was sixteen, she said we were leaving for a civilized place or she'd go insane.

"I've seen it happen to women before. Sometimes the land snatches away their joy in life. I didn't want to be civilized, so I stayed here. My ma took off for San Francisco…I can't blame her for it. She's remarried and living the life of a fine lady, just like she always dreamed of. We write to each other now and then."

"You're a lucky man, Matt. You had your mother for a time. Even now you have her letters. I was raised by other people's mothers."

It was comfortable talking to Matt. Maybe their time together would pass pleasantly, in friendship. The ruckus down in town seemed to grow distant on this peaceful porch in the dead of night. Conversation and moonlight made everything feel right.

"I never knew my real ma or pa. I think I was born in New York. I showed up in a basket on some church steps. I was cared for by an older couple. They raised me for as long as they could, but in the end I wound up on an orphan train. I was seven then."

While she spoke, Matt reached over and took her hand. He folded it inside both of his big, rough fists and rubbed his thumb over her knuckles.

"I'm sure sorry about that," he murmured.

"I got along. I'd go to a family and do what work I could in exchange for what shelter and affection they were able to give. I grew and changed families a few times before I was old enough to be on my own and get paid for the work I did.

"Now I've finally got a place of my own. With what I make on Orange Lilly I can sink in my roots and never have to move on again." As long as Dr. Coonley continued producing patent medicine and the railroads continued delivering to Dodge, she ought to have a dependable income.

"Darlin', I'm going to build you the finest house around. Those wandering days of yours are gone for good." Matt stood. He kept hold of her hand and drew her up with him. Lands, if his touch wasn't the most tender thing she'd ever felt. "I think it's about time for us to head on up to bed."

Lordy! There was only one bed in his room.

All the way up the steps to the second floor he kept hold of her hand. A lucky thing, too, since visions of what could happen on that one bed drained the strength right out of her legs. Blamed if she didn't feel heat twisting in her secret places.

Once inside the room with the door closed, Emma shook herself. Not a thing was going to happen on the bed with Lucy curled in the middle of it.

Matt leaned into the circle of moonlight surrounding

his daughter and kissed the top of her head. He straightened, then shot Emma a smile slanted in mischief.

"I'll step into Red's room if you need a moment to slip into your sleeping gown." The hint of a dimple creasing his cheek told her that this was a challenge more than a genuine offer.

"I believe that dressing screen in the corner should provide all the modesty a married lady needs," she said, and wondered if it would.

She stepped behind it and took off her dress and underclothes. In spite of her casual words, she didn't feel at all modest. The shifting and twisting in her belly made her hope that he could see through the screen.

Mercy, with the way he was staring at it, maybe he could! Moonlight whispering through the window glanced off her naked skin. What stood in the way of making this marriage real, besides the child in the bed? Just her desire to live alone? She lifted her arms and let down her hair. She drew her fingers through it to make it loose and fluffy.

She thought she heard Matt gasp and peeked over the top of the screen. He'd plopped down on the edge of the bed.

"You sure you can't see through this screen?" Hopefully she sounded more chaste than she felt.

"If I were you I'd finish up quick."

Emma turned and lifted the lid of her trunk. She drew out her nightgown and ever so slowly let it slide down her body. How wanton of her was it to imagine that the fabric gliding over her breasts was Matt's calloused hand?

After one more toss of her hair, she stepped from behind the screen.

"Your turn," she said lightly to cover her true yearnings.

Matt stood up from the bed when Emma crawled between the wall and Lucy to snuggle down onto the mattress.

"Every time I think I've got you figured out, you surprise the hell out of me," he whispered.

She'd certainly surprised the hell out of herself. If it weren't for Lucy lying smack in the center of the bed, Emma might have ripped this gown right off.

The strange urge didn't ease any when Matt didn't go behind the screen to get undressed. He faced her with a lock of hair brushing the deepening crease in his cheek, unbuttoned his shirt and slid it off. He hung it over the screen, then untied the scarf from around his neck and draped it over the shirt.

She'd seen men remove their shirts for farm work or field chores, but she'd never wanted to reach out and touch any of them. Maybe it was the moonlight painting Matt's muscles in strokes of bronze and silver that made her fingers itch.

Maybe it was the fact that she was his legally wedded wife and could reach out with a nearly clear conscience that made her breath quicken under the sheets.

When her husband dropped his jeans and crawled under the covers wearing only red drawers, she felt the need to hold her breath to keep from groaning.

Mercy, how was she going to make it through the rest of the summer like this? Surely Lucy wouldn't be sleeping between them every night.

Fantasies of Matt's hard bronzed body settling over hers, with his sun-kissed hair swooping down to tickle her neck and his lips tasting places that had never been tasted, had Emma floating on a cloud of pure delight.

As if sensing her feelings, Matt reached over Lucy's head and grasped Emma's hand where it lay on the pillow near her head. He twined his fingers through hers and let them lie bound together, silk and leather.

A smile teased the corners of his mouth. Across the moonlit bed Emma yearned to kiss it. Married was married after all.

Suddenly Lawrence Pendragon's voice shot out of a corner of her memory.

"What's wrong, Emma?" He squeezed her hand. The smile vanished from his face. "We won't do anything you don't want to."

"Who is Angus Hawker?"

The breath came out of Matt's lungs in a long whoosh. He glanced at Lucy and touched her cheek, apparently testing the depth of her sleep.

Even though Lucy didn't stir, he spoke in a whisper. "What did you hear about him?"

"That he is going to kill you."

"That's his plan, all right."

"But why?"

"Do you recall what I told you about coming upon Red?"

"You did what needed to be done to save Red's life."

Matt hugged his fingers tighter about hers. "I killed a man. The fellow that Red was facing was hot for a fight, and not going to settle for less than a quick draw, so I obliged him. His name was Seth Hawker. Angus is his brother. Angus was in prison when the shooting happened, but he'll be out by summer's end. I figure he'll make it to Dodge by early fall."

Emma's heart seemed to be tumbling in midair. The thought of her handsome husband, no matter how recently she had come by him, lying cold in a grave made tears strain at the back of her eyes.

He braced himself up on one elbow to peer down at her face.

"There's something I need to explain to you." He let go of her hand to feather the outline of her hair, but he clenched his fist instead of touching it. "I could pick up Lucy and carry her over to Red's room. That's what I want to do. I never meant to be married, but darlin', in just one day you've got me rethinking that. If I was free to do it, I'd press you back on this bed and bind you to me."

"I might not mind being bound, for now."

Matt bent over Lucy and kissed Emma lightly on the lips.

"Hell's fire, woman, you'd be sorry within the week. But the truth is, it can't be that way for us. I've got to take Red and Lucy and ride for California before Hawker gets here."

Of course he did. She only prayed that the tear breaking loose from her eye didn't make him think that she felt otherwise.

"I won't leave until I get your house built, that's a promise." Emma couldn't help but reach up and brush the brown-sugar hair sweeping alongside his cheek back behind his ear. "You are some kind of woman, darlin'. Maybe even the kind who can make it out here."

Matt eased down onto his side of the bed. He took her hand again and twined his fingers in hers. This time he laid them over the rise and fall of Lucy's small rib cage.

"I wouldn't go away if I didn't think so."

Mercy, wouldn't a body who'd just been handed everything she wanted be bursting at the seams for joy? Just her and Pearl out on their land with no one to care for had been her wish for years on end.

Now all of a sudden the thought didn't give her the thrill it once had. Surely in the morning after a good night's sleep it would come back fresh, but for now all she wanted was to lie in the dark and feel like Matt's wife.

Chapter Five

Keeping a dugout clean was work enough to make a woman scream. Since Emma didn't want the men outside to figure her for a weakling, she hummed a tune that anyone would think was cheerful.

A beam of sunshine shot through the open dugout door and illuminated the bed that she shared with Lucy. She smoothed the covers flat, then flicked away a flea that fell from the dirt ceiling.

If it weren't for the bugs living in her walls, the soddie would be pleasant enough. She'd lined the walls with fabrics and covered the floor with canvas. Cool during the day and warm at night, it was a snug retreat from the wind and sun. Even at midnight, the only wild creature she needed to worry about was of the insect variety.

The men preferred to sleep outside near the campfire that burned day and night. It was what they were used to, they claimed. It reminded them of being on the roundup.

Evidently Matt preferred outdoor life, as well. Lucy and Emma had slept alone for the full two weeks they had been here.

It was only midmorning and Emma had swept the dugout floor twice, but she snatched up the broom and did it again.

For the moment, her home was clean enough for her to do a job she had wanted to begin for ever so long. This morning she would plant trees. Matt had met the train yesterday and picked up her order of fruit trees along with her shipment of Orange Lilly.

It had pleased her no end that Matt had returned to the homestead with half the case of Orange Lilly sold and ten dollars in his pocket. The crease in his cheek had been flashing when he'd told her that five ladies from town had approached the wagon before he'd turned off Front Street, vowing they would perish if he didn't sell them the snake oil.

Emma filled a basket with chicken, bread and a piece of peach pie left over from last night. She took a canteen from a peg on the wall and put it in with the food.

She plucked her bonnet from the corner where her clothes hung and took Lucy's little one, as well. The child didn't care for her hat, never having been required to wear one before. It was clear that the men who'd raised her doted on the girl. What a shame they'd never thought to protect her fair face from sunburn.

No doubt at this very moment Lucy splashed in the creek like a little boy, heedless of the sun beating down and turning her skin pink.

Emma closed the heavy wood door that Matt had installed on the dugout the first day here. At least it would keep the prairie soot from getting in until she opened the door again.

As always, when Emma stepped outside her heart skipped over itself. Every day the lumber pile in the yard grew smaller. A little more than a cow's bellow away from the creek, fresh-smelling wood took the shape of a home.

A body would think she'd get used to seeing it. Still, every time she spotted Matt carrying a heavy piece of lumber or driving home a nail, her pulse quickened. She'd always known she'd love her new home.

Five men labored in the early-morning heat. Cousin Billy and Jesse worked on the house, Red on the barn. Except that just now Red was watching Lucy by the creek. Matt stood by the well in the shade of the roof he had built over it. He spoke with a man he had hired, Rusty Cohen, an experienced home builder in Dodge.

Matt and Rusty looked up from their conversation when they spotted her coming toward the well. Rusty tipped his hat. A grin that made her insides weak slid across Matt's face.

Sometime before summer's end she would have to learn not to enjoy it so much.

"I left some lunch in the dugout." Emma took the canteen from the basket. When she reached for the ladle in the bucket Matt took it from her and filled the canteen.

"Are you wearing those new boots?" he asked.

Since Rusty had glanced down at her feet, she raised the hem of her gown only enough for the toe of one leather boot to peek out. When Matt had presented them to her she had yanked her skirt up past her knee, aglow with the impropriety of it.

"I wouldn't want to meet the snake that could sink its fangs through this leather," she said.

"All the same," Matt said and tucked the filled canteen into the basket. "I had Red look the area over when he dropped off your trees. It seemed clear at the time, but you'd better keep an eye out."

"There's no need to worry about Lucy and me. We're on Parker land."

Rusty arched his heavy brows and tipped his head. Matt took the revolver from his holster and tucked it in with the canteen.

"Don't shoot at anything unless you have to. Just point the gun out toward the horizon and I'll come running."

Emma didn't like the feel of a loaded weapon in her picnic basket. Wouldn't a scream get attention as easily as gunfire?

She rose on her toes to kiss Matt's cheek. She'd only just realized her slip of the tongue in calling her homestead Parker land instead of Suede land. This casual display of wifely affection toward her husband should smooth that over.

"Good day, Mr. Cohen," Emma said, then headed toward the corral where Pearl nuzzled noses with Thunder.

"Come on, Pearl, we're going for a walk."

The horse whinnied and trotted toward the corral gate. Emma didn't bother with tack equipment, since she wouldn't be riding the horse. Pearl followed behind Emma swishing her tail while they walked toward the creek to fetch Lucy.

After a moment of disagreement over wearing the bonnet, Lucy allowed Emma to tie up the ribbons under her chin in exchange for riding to the site of the tree-planting on Pearl's bare back.

Surely too soon for Lucy, Emma lifted her from the horse.

"Here we are. Which tree do you want to plant first?" Lucy raced toward the row of thirty trees that Red had set in a line. "This one!"

"That's a fine choice. It's an apple." Emma picked up the sapling. "Let's plant it right here in front so we can see it from the house."

Emma set the picnic basket with the loaded gun well away from the area where they would be working. From what she had learned of youngsters, they seemed to be attracted to the very thing that would cause them grief.

She found a shovel in the pile of tools that Red had left behind with the trees.

"Put it here, Mama." Lucy jumped up and down on the spot of prairie she had picked for her tree. "I want it right here where Mr. Hoppety can come and get an apple."

There might not be enough apples for all the Mr. Hoppetys in the creek, but the place looked as good as any to begin.

Emma expected the sod to be hard digging. She'd heard the tales of sodbusters truly being busted over it. To her amazement, the shovel went in as if it was cutting into cake.

She'd have to bake something special for whichever one of Matt's gang had thought to prepare the ground.

With the hole dug, she knelt beside it and set the tree in. Matt's big gloves nearly slipped off her hands while she pressed the dirt around the roots, filling the hole.

"What do you say we give your tree a name?"

Lucy plopped down on her knees. She pressed her hands on top of Emma's firming the dirt. "I want to call it Hoppety."

"Next thing, you'll want to turn your name to Hoppety." Lucy giggled. Childish laughter was one of the things Emma liked most. She reached for Lucy's middle and tickled. "Hoppety, Hoppety, Hoppety!"

Lucy's giggles rang out over the land. Pearl quit her grazing to let out a playful snort.

"Hoppety Suede!"

"Mama, I'm Lucy!" she declared with a hiccup.

"Yes, you are. I suppose your papa wouldn't like it if you turned into a frog." Lucy shook her head hard. She'd quit laughing when the tickling ended, but her eyes continued to dance with blue sparkles. Healthy children had the most wonderful glow about them. "Lucy, sweetheart, you know that I'm not really your mama, don't you?"

"You brush my hair like a real ma, and make me wear a bonnet."

"I think you're a fine little girl." Emma touched Lucy's chin and peered into a face that had grown suddenly solemn. "Someday you'll have a real mama and that's what you'll want to call her."

"I want to call you Mama."

"How about if you call me Mama Emma?"

The sparkle flashed back into Lucy's eyes. She hugged Emma tightly around the neck.

Hopefully she hadn't set Lucy up for heartache by giving in to that name.

"We'd better get busy giving the rest of these trees names."

Lucy let go of her neck and hurried over to the line of trees lying on the ground.

"This one is Lucy." She pointed to a peach tree and then to a pecan. "This one is Mama Emma."

Lordy, she'd never allowed a child to call her Mama-anything. She prayed that she wouldn't have to mend that mistake at summer's end.

After two hours, Emma and Lucy broke for lunch. Emma took the gun out of the picnic basket and set it beside the tools.

After they'd eaten, Lucy yawned, stretched and fell asleep on the picnic blanket.

"Come on over here, Pearl." Emma positioned the horse so that her shadow covered Lucy. "That's a good horse. Now, don't move. Stay right there."

Pearl whickered and nuzzled Emma's chin.

"I'd best get back to work on these trees. In no time at all I'll be feeding you apples from them." She kissed Pearl's velvety muzzle. "You watch over Hoppety there, and I'll bake you a pie full of apples."

It took only another hour to get the remaining trees into the ground, thanks to the soil preparation that must have taken such time and sweat.

She firmed the dirt around the last sapling. The bawling of a steer cut the peaceful afternoon. Mercy, if it didn't seem to be right behind her.

Emma pivoted on her knees. A bull munched Hoppety Tree between his hairy brown jaws. Dirt crumbled from the roots before the huge mouth chomped and swallowed them.

"Shoo!" She jumped up and waved her apron at him. "Go away!"

"I wouldn't wave your clothing at him, ma'am."

Emma glanced up to see a cowboy ride into view. "If this beast belongs to you, get him off my land!"

"Now, the trouble with beasts is that they don't have a speck of respect for property lines."

Finished with Hoppety Tree, the bull lumbered toward the next tree in line. The cowboy gave him an indulgent smile.

"You get this steak off my property, Mr...."

"Mr. Samuel Tucker, foreman for Lawrence Pendragon." The cowboy twirled a rope over his head and lassoed the bull but he let it hang slack, giving the animal the space he needed to eat another tree.

"Fickle critters." Mr. Tucker drew his gun from his holster and aimed it at the munching steer.

"You never know what they're going to do." While he spoke, the barrel of his gun shifted. It took dead aim on Lucy asleep in Pearl's shade.

Angry heat flashed through Emma. She stepped between the piece and the child.

Blast! Why had she left Matt's gun with the pile of tools? A good twenty feet lay between her and the weapon. She took a few sidesteps in that direction.

Praise be! The cowboy's gun shifted away from Lucy and toward her. The sun's glare glinted up and down the length of it.

Pearl snorted. She lowered her head to sniff Lucy then stepped over her so that she straddled her. The good horse had always had a sense for protecting young ones.

"I've seen these cattle trample the dreams of many a settler," the foreman declared.

So far, the cowboy hadn't wrapped his finger around the trigger of his revolver. Emma stopped to consider her situation further. Even if she made it to Matt's gun, what then? The cattleman had the upper hand, since he already had a weapon pointed at her heart.

If she could get on the far side of the big red steer,

she'd be safer. The man might think twice about shooting his boss's livestock.

"Yep, I couldn't tell you the times I've seen the ornery cusses hurt or even kill folks who got in their way."

"Why, you low-down, flea in a dog's—"

A shotgun blast blew away the meanest thing Emma had ever said to anyone. The gun flew out of the foreman's hand as if a twister had snatched it away.

The startled steer made a run toward Pearl, but the blind horse stood her ground. She lowered her head and snorted. The steer turned and bolted across the prairie with the rope snaking behind him.

Emma spun about to see where the shot had come from.

Matt stood halfway between the new house and the place where she had planted her trees.

He kept the rifle trained on Mr. Tucker while he walked forward. The prairie breeze lifted the hair trailing out from under his hat. The sun shone off his jeans with each long stride he took.

"Tucker, you've known me for a long time." Matt stood at the edge of the turned earth with the rifle's aim settled on the foreman. "You know I could have blown away a whole lot more than your sidearm."

Matt never lowered his aim. He stood steady with his legs braced wide and his vest rippling in the wind. "Turn around and ride that pony hard. You'd best make it your personal business to be sure Pendragon's beeves stay clear of my land."

Tucker shot Matt a sullen look, but he turned his horse and trotted after the steer.

With the danger past, Emma became aware of

Lucy's sobs. The shotgun blast must have woken her with an awful scare.

Good old Pearl stood guard. She lowered her muzzle to Lucy and nickered at her hair.

Emma reached Lucy a step before Matt did. She swept her up in a comforting hug.

"It's all right, baby." Lucy snuggled her face into Emma's neck. "It's all right."

Matt stroked Lucy's back, but his gaze following Tucker's retreat toward the Pendragon spread told her that everything was far from all right.

Thunder rumbled in the distance, but Matt figured the rain to be still some way off. There'd be another hour of sitting outside by the campfire before they'd all be driven into the dugout for the night.

The scene set out about him looked as cozy as anything he'd ever seen. Lucy slept in the dugout, a tuckered-out jumping bean, Jesse had gone back to the livery for the night and Rusty had gone home, but Emma, Red and Billy sat with him under the gathering clouds soaking up the cheer of the fire.

He needed some cheer. The threat that Pendragon had sent over this afternoon had him sitting uneasy. The man kept the marshal in his back pocket and pretty much ran free rein over the town. Matt had seen the things that happened to settlers who defied the powerful foreigner.

Emma would be safe for as long as he could act the part of her husband, but what would happen come autumn?

It struck him that it might be a fine thing for her to

find a respectable man, one who would stand up for her once he'd gone. It struck him like a fist in the gut!

Matt sipped his coffee and watched her across the flames. He'd ripped his shirt before dinner tonight and now that shirt lay in Emma's lap, as he wished he could do. Her delicate-looking fingers worked a needle in and out of the fabric in what seemed to him to be a caress. Firelight bronzed her skin and sparkled on the needle.

He sure would like to make up a song about the honey glow of her hair and the pretty way her lips puckered together while she concentrated on her mending.

In the end it would be best to let that song go. The singing of it later on might weigh too heavily on his heart.

When the time came, he needed to be able to ride off with no more than a friendly wave goodbye between them.

Out across the prairie thunder rolled and bucked, but it was still far enough off that they could remain gathered about the fire.

Red laughed out loud. The knife he used to carve a toy for Lucy went still while he listened to some story that Billy told. The words were low and whispered. It must be some sort of tale that they would have told out loud without Emma there to hear it.

Coffee and firelight spun a nice web around the four of them and created one of those moments a man wanted to pluck out of time to savor again later. But the air had begun to smell damp and no magic could last forever.

Matt poured another cup of coffee, then closed his eyes to listen to the night sounds. Crickets chirruped close at hand and far off a steer bellowed. The wind picked up and set the prairie grass whispering.

Over the crackle and sparking of the flames he imagined he heard the gentle rise and fall of Emma's breathing and the slip of her needle through his shirt.

"If it was me, I'd have shot him clean off his horse." Red's whisper carried across the fire. Emma's needle stopped midstitch.

"That's because you don't have the sense that God gave a buffalo chip," Cousin Billy said.

"He had it coming, pointing the gun at Emma like that. Matt could have sent him along to hell, and he should have."

Sometimes Red scared the boots right off Matt. Red was almost an echo of himself at that age. He had the look of a man, but inside he was as green as the saplings Emma had planted down near the creek.

"You shouldn't talk about a man's life with such disregard, son," Matt said.

"He wasn't showing any regard for Emma and Lucy this afternoon. Any man who tries to shoot a helpless woman and child is no better than a cow pile. He doesn't deserve to walk the earth."

Matt dumped the rest of his coffee into the fire. All of a sudden it didn't set well in his belly.

"I'd have to agree with the cow-pile part, but it's not for you to decide who deserves to walk the earth."

"Someone needs to make sure criminals get their due."

"Unless you're planning to take the marshal's job, it's not you. Until you can recognize whether a man is out to do murder or just mischief, you keep that gun of yours in its leather."

"I saw what I saw."

"You saw a mean-spirited threat and nothing more.

Even though Sam Tucker is lower than a maggot on a carcass, it's not for you to decide his fate."

"Billy the Kid wouldn't have let him go."

"Billy the Kid is dead."

Red shot to his feet. He'd always had a foolish hero image of the killer that Matt had never been able to dissuade him from.

"You made that up!"

"Pat Garrett gunned him down one night last week. It came in over the wire last time I was in town."

Red stomped off with anger and rebellion in his stride. A bolt of lightning split the sky overhead and a fat warm drop of water hit Matt on the nose. He jumped up and caught up with Red in a few long strides.

"Red." He grasped the boy's arm and spun him around. "Any man who chooses to live by the gun finds an early grave. I've seen it happen time and again. I'll be damned if I'm going to see it happen to you."

"Nothing's going to happen to me." All at once the rain crashed down. Red dashed for the dugout and vanished in a blur of water.

The realization that the nervous lowing of cattle and the snap of a cowboy's whip was not a dream came to Matt like fog gradually lifting off the land. A shrill whistle made him bolt up from his pallet on the floor

The distant noise was so muffled by rain that Matt believed he was the only one to have noticed it—until he glanced at Emma's bed. Although the darkness inside was nearly complete, the open dugout door let in enough illumination for him to make out a single tiny form beneath the covers of his wife's bed.

"Damnation, woman," he muttered under his breath.

With a penny's worth of luck she'd only made a trip to the outhouse, but more than likely she'd gone to investigate the sounds of cattle roaming where they shouldn't.

Matt jammed his feet into his boots, thanking his stars that he'd decided to sleep in his clothes the way he did on the nights spent under the open sky. On the way out the door he grabbed his gun belt. He fastened it around his hips on a run toward the stir of unsettled cattle.

The land between the house and the creek sloped gently downward. It gave him an unobstructed view of the acre devoted to Emma's trees.

Three mounted cowboys whipped and whistled a good fifty head of cattle across the creek. The storm-spooked animals trampled the trees that Emma had spent the day putting in the ground. Not a single green leaf showed beneath the clumsy beeves' hooves. The planting field had turned into an acre mud puddle. Matt didn't doubt that the cowboys had intentionally pushed the cattle so that every one of the trees lay buried in the muck.

A streak of white flashed against the mud-soaked land. It was Emma dashing to the rescue of her damned orchard! Even under the deluge of rain, Matt felt the cold sweat of fear break out on his skin. Did she think she could scare the beasts off by yelling and waving at them?

Anger shot out of his brain like nothing he'd ever felt. Those men of Pendragon's had to see her running toward the herd, and yet they continued to whip them up.

Matt reached for his gun but let his hand lie tense

and loose beside it. A gunshot might be just the thing
to send the herd into a full-blown panic.

"Emma! Get back!" He knew she wouldn't hear over
the storm and the cattle. Even if she did, odds were even
that she'd ignore his order.

"Thunder!" Matt let go a shrill whistle. The stallion
pranced about his corral. He circled twice, then sailed
over the fence.

The horse caught up with him in only a few seconds.
He caught its mane and hauled himself up on the slick
back without missing a step. A well-trained and fearless
pony was the best friend a cowboy could have.

He was still a hundred yards off when Pendragon's
men spotted him. He must have looked like the devil
coming down, for they turned on their mounts and lit
off toward home.

If only his wife had such sense. She had run right
into the throng of beeves, shooing them with the soaked
hem of her nightgown. Memories of Utah's broken body
made his gut heave and twist.

"Get out! Go away!" He was close enough now to
hear her scream at them. A huge brown bull lowered
his head and pawed at the ground. Emma flapped her
nightgown.

It wasn't necessary to direct Thunder in what needed
to be done. The horse kicked up a wall of mud weaving
in and out of the cattle, making his way toward Emma.

Matt leaned low over Thunder's back, blinking back
mud and spitting it off his lips. The stallion's bare back
was too wet and slippery to catch Emma up as he would
do in the solid leather of a saddle.

Thunder must have sensed that. He halted in front of
Emma, using his living bulk as a shield. Matt reached

down and pulled her up in front of him at the instant the bull began his charge. As soon as Emma's weight hit his back the stallion dashed into the center of the herd.

A good horse was better than a friend. He could mean the difference between life and death.

The bull, confused at losing sight of its target, became just one more jittery steer.

Matt urged the horse toward the outer edge of the herd on them. He drew his gun and fired in the air. Between the gunshots and Thunder's running herd, the cattle retreated to familiar ground.

With the beeves in retreat, Matt exhaled a pent-up breath of relief. He tugged one arm tighter around Emma's waist then bent his head to her shoulder. Rain sluiced between his cheek and her neck.

"Good God, Emma. Where's your sense? Those cattle were spooked and dangerous."

A shudder that probably didn't have a thing to do with the rain rippled over her skin. Matt rubbed his hands up and down her bare arms to smooth it away.

"I was so angry, I didn't think."

"Darlin', you've got to think about every move you make out here. This isn't like town where help's right next door and the doc just up the block."

Emma let out a deep sigh and laid her head back against Matt's shoulder. Her neck arched backward, and sodden hair clung to bare flesh. All of a sudden Matt was the one not doing the thinking.

The scent of womanly skin, damp and steamy, filled his nose and boiled his brain. Her soaked nightgown might as well have been packed in her trunk in the dugout for all the modesty it provided. He'd have had to be a saint to keep from watching the rise and fall of her breasts, full and glistening with the rain and her heavy breathing.

No one had ever accused him of being a saint.

He might have touched them, he might have quieted her fluttering heart with a stroke of his fingertips if he hadn't heard Red and Billy yelling and running toward the smashed orchard.

Emma's clinging nightgown might be fit for a husband's eyes, but he'd be damned if Red or Billy would get a glimpse of it.

"Nothing to be done here tonight, boys. Go back inside and mind Lucy."

Billy waved his arm in acknowledgment and yanked on Red's sleeve, making sure that the boy followed.

Evidently Emma didn't agree that there was nothing to be done. She slid off Thunder's back, apparently unaware that her gown hadn't slid with her. The glimpse of a gleaming thigh and the curve of a pearly nether cheek nearly knocked him off Thunder's back.

Emma knelt in the mud and dug her fingers in deep. She found a ball of roots with a trunk still attached to it.

"What are you doing?" Matt scooted off Thunder and stood over Emma's bent back. Rain beat down and washed the sapling's trunk, revealing the damage.

"Planting what I can of these trees."

She tried to dig a hole, but it filled with water nearly as fast as she could dig. Matt knelt beside her.

"Not now." He caught her hands to hold them still. He felt the anger and the cold shaking her fingers. "Tomorrow we'll go to town and order new trees."

She slipped free of his grasp and snatched up the tree with the roots still on. "These are my trees. Lucy and I named every last one of them. No low-down no-good is going to take them from me."

"That's just not reasonable, Emma darlin'. They won't live with being trampled on. Besides, we'll catch our deaths out here."

"Let the boys know that breakfast might be late."

If God had ever created a more stubborn woman, he hadn't heard tell of her. She lifted a mud-caked hand to wipe the hair out of her face. A brown smear streaked across her cheek. The rain washed it down the constricting muscles of her throat.

She wanted to cry—it was plain as anything—but instead she plopped the wounded tree into the ground, then plunged her hands into the muck in search of another.

Blamed if his wife didn't have the grit of a dozen men.

Matt took off his shirt and settled it over her shoulders before he plunged his hands into the liquid sod in search of a battered, hopeless tree.

Chapter Six

Emma hung a wet pair of jeans on the line to dry. A drop of wash water rolled down her wrist, sparkling in the August sunshine. Nearly two weeks had passed since Matt had knelt in the mud beside her, replanting trees that he knew good and well would not survive.

What had survived from that night was the memory of Matt squatting bare chested in the mud with rain washing over his skin. Lands, if she hadn't wanted to toss her tree aside and run her fingers across his glistening back.

Good common sense had been no more than a lightning bolt away from being dumped in the mud. Indeed, she had been reaching toward him ready to trace his flexing muscles with her mud-caked fingers when lightning had flashed a shocking blue-white glare over her ruined field.

She'd reined in that honey-slick impulse before Matt had known what she was about, but for the past two weeks she'd been wondering what might have happened if she hadn't.

"Mama Emma, lift me up." Lucy waved a small wet

calico dress that she had taken from the laundry pile. "I want to hang up my own."

"Okay, sweetie—jump high when I lift you." The leap took a considerable bit of weight off the task. "Hook the pins right at the shoulder...there, good girl."

"Let me do another one." Evidently, to Lucy, laundry hanging was a morning game.

"Just once more." Lucy jumped, Emma lifted. "I swear you get bigger each time I pick you up."

As soon as her tiny boots touched the ground, she wrapped her arms around Emma's thigh and hugged tight.

"I don't want to get a new ma someday." She gazed up past Emma's apron with eyes so solemn they looked like the sky with a storm gathering. "I want you to be my mama till I'm all grown up."

Lordy, how she wished she could fall on her knees and hug that child up tight to her bosom. Somehow, living alone didn't have the sparkle it once had. Lately she found herself having to look deeper in her heart to find the thrill of being independent.

In the end it didn't matter how she felt. That outlaw was going to come gunning for Matt. He would take his family and move to California.

"I can't be your mama for that long, baby, but I can always be your friend."

"You can be my ma if you want to."

How was a body to explain to a little girl how impossible that was? Luckily she was spared that by the sudden appearance of a green-wheeled buggy coming over a rise of ground.

The ever-blowing wind stirred up a gust of dust that

would have to be brushed out of the clothes when they dried.

"Somebody's here!" Lucy dashed off to greet the approaching wagon.

When the wagon pulled in front of the now fully framed house, Mrs. Sizeloff waved. Charlie jumped down from the wagon.

Emma reached the buggy and Mrs. Sizeloff handed down a basket with her baby, Maudie, asleep inside.

Praise be that there was always a pot of coffee going for the men. With the scones left over from breakfast, she could treat her guest to a proper welcome.

They sat on the floor of the framed house with the breeze blowing through, eating scones and drinking coffee.

Mrs. Sizeloff didn't seem to mind the lack of chairs while they spoke of this and that going on in town. She'd come for a supply of Orange Lilly for herself and her sister in Kinsley who had frightful monthlies.

"I spoke with your husband when he came to town to buy a load of barbed wire. He told me about the troubles you've had with those wandering cattle."

"It's not the cattle so much as their owner that's giving me grief." Emma swallowed the last sip of coffee from her mug and set it down. "Why, that Mr. Pendragon must think he's king, wanting everybody's land right along with his own."

"It wouldn't hurt to see him sitting beside his daughter in church more on a Sunday.... Charlie!" she called out to her son, who splashed in the creek with Lucy. "Go get what we brought in the wagon and bring it up here to the house."

Charlie pounded barefoot past the house, then scrambled up onto the wagon. He returned with a pair of squirming, whining puppies, one tucked under each arm.

"We had a litter of ten a few months past." Rachael Sizeloff took one of the pups from Charlie and set it in Emma's lap. "I thought Pendragon might not sneak up on you so easily with these two to announce him. Their mother is as fine a dog as God ever made."

A pair of pups would be demanding but, mercy, they might be just the companions she would need after Matt and Lucy had gone.

"Aren't they sweet?" Emma breathed in a lungful of puppy scent, then handed the dog to Lucy. "Feel how soft he is. Maybe you can give him a name."

Lucy held the pup the way she held her rag doll. Evidently it didn't take to being toted about like a hunk of cotton. It twisted and wiggled until it got free, then ran toward the creek with Lucy only a stride behind.

"Thank you, Mrs. Sizeloff. Once they get some size on them they ought to be a help."

Mrs. Sizeloff stood, stretched, then called for Charlie.

"Time to be on our way. The Williamses have a sick baby. We can only hope it isn't the cholera. I need to take my young ones to Mrs. Conner so Josie and I can go on over and sit with the poor parents and watch in prayer."

"Let me get that Orange Lilly for you."

Emma hurried toward the dugout to get the patent medicine. If only it worked on the cholera. She'd heard of too many children taken by the sickness.

The thought of losing Lucy that way made her feel

weak in the knees. Maybe she was closer to being the mother that Lucy dreamed of than she realized.

"This fence ought to make Pendragon as mad as a swatted bee," Billy said while he unwound several feet of barbed wire.

"As dangerous as a loco bull, too." Matt hammered the sharp wire into place.

He knew that they were waving a red flag in front of the man. Being dangerous and angry weren't good things to encourage in the Englishman. It would be better to stay on the man's good side, which still meant he was an arrogant cuss, but not so likely to do harm.

"Good thing you brought back plenty of wire," Billy said. "We'll be fixing cut fences from now until kingdom come."

"Until fall, anyway."

"What about after that?" Billy took off his hat and wiped the sweat from his face with his sleeve. "What's Emma going to do about Pendragon once we've gone?"

That was a question that had left Matt gazing at the stars more than the backs of his eyelids at night. A woman needed a man out here on the plains, no matter how much she didn't think so. Emma might be a pistol, she might be as spirited a woman as he'd ever laid eyes on, but she would be no match for the sodbusting life and Pendragon together.

"As I see it, you can do one of two things, cousin." Billy hammered a section of wire into place. "First thing, and best thing, is to get her to come along to California."

"You'd better tell me the other one. You see the way

she moons about that new house. I'd have to hog-tie her to the train to get her to leave the place."

"I don't see any help for it, then, but to find her a new man." Billy kept his eyes focused on his task, pounding in a nail and unrolling another length of wire. "A good strapping fellow who can hold things together in your place."

Another man in his place? The thought made him mad enough to spit the nails into the fence.

"You crazy fool, a man doesn't give away his wife."

"A man doesn't sleep outside with a pair of smelly cowboys when his wife's lying clean and sweet inside the dugout, either."

"A man doesn't make holy bonds of that sort unless he's planning on being around. Hell, Billy, you know I can't stay here—there's Lucy and Red to consider." Matt dropped his hammer and picked up his canteen. He took a long swallow, then splashed some water on his face. "Could be that you're waiting to step into my place."

"That would suit me just fine if I was the marrying kind."

Matt started to declare that he wasn't the marrying kind, either, but Billy had been able to read his lies since they were eight years old.

"A man never knows when he might get to be the marrying kind. It might come to him right out of the blue," Matt said.

"It doesn't take a voyeur to see what's hit you out of the blue. And it's no wonder. I suppose we've all gone a little soft for Emma in our own ways. But all that aside, with Hawker getting out, you've got to go and Emma needs a man."

Wasn't that the worry that had kept him awake night after restless night?

"I suppose you have my replacement picked out?"

"Woody Vance."

Matt's stomach turned sour on his breakfast. Woody Vance was a tall, husky fellow who felt a call to the land nearly as strong as Emma did. The man also felt a call to Emma. Evidently Cousin Billy hadn't missed the way the farmer had gazed after Emma the times they had been in town.

Matt retrieved his hammer from the ground and smashed a nail into the wood post harder than he needed to.

"I suppose you've thought of a way to get me replaced?"

"I do a lot of thinking while I'm working." Billy walked toward the next post, dragging the wire with him. "As I see it, we'll have a party to celebrate the new house being finished. With all the dancing and merriment going on, they ought to take to each other like butterflies in a field."

"You've got a mind for writing dime novels. I'm not handing my wife over to the first farmer who comes along."

"I'm just saying Woody could take care of her once we've gone."

Woody Vance was young, strong and fine to look at from a woman's eye. It hurt to dwell on the ways he might take care of her.

Matt was spared having to consider it further when he looked up and saw Emma bringing lunch. She rode Pearl with Lucy nestled in front of her and a pair of

"You know I can't do that." But he did touch her. With both his hands. Her heart beat triple time under his fingers.

"I was angry when I made you promise that. We don't have much time left." She rubbed her fingertips in a circle around his nipples, so he did the same to her.

She moaned something, maybe his name. "Please, be my husband for a little while."

"I can't, not for a little while. It's got to be for good."

"I can't give you for good, Matt. You can't give it to me, either."

Matt put his arms about her and rolled, setting her beside him then drawing them both down, side by side in the grass.

He leaned up on his elbow. Moonlight kissed Emma. It twinkled her cheeks, laughed along her neck, then stroked shimmers across her chest and ribs. It pooled in the hollow between her hips, then fingered down to tease her mound of woman's hair. It adored her like the luckiest of lovers. He wished life would allow him to do the same.

"What if I stayed?"

"Don't tease me."

"If I told you I would, we'd have a big whoop-de-do over it and ruin this." He gestured toward the water, the sky and their naked bodies.

She scrunched up on her shoulder, looking at him, eye to eye. "We would. If you said those words, our fight would wake the children who are likely tucked in bed at the party by now."

"If I asked you to come to California?"

"That would wake the folks in Dodge." She stroked his hair, his cheek with the back of her hand. "If I asked you to make love to me, just forget about what's coming, what then?"

"Could you be so cruel, darlin'? To take my heart, then toss it back to me when I'm leaving?" Lord, he hadn't wanted her to well up. A fight might have been better. He dashed the moisture off her cheek. "Looks like we're at an impasse. You can't go my way and I can't go yours."

"We have tonight. Let's call a truce. Just this once, we put it all aside. What if we lie here until morning with nothing between us but moonlight."

"I suppose we can have that fight tomorrow."

She lay back on the grass. He did the same. Emma reached for his hand at the same instant he reached for hers.

Back home an hour before dawn and still in her party dress, Emma stood in her kitchen. Set out on the table, slowly plumping in the lamplight, were six loaves of rising dough. She gave each one a punch in the center and watched while the warm dough folded in on itself.

Was she cruel? Maybe even selfish? If she looked at things through Matt's eyes, maybe.

It had been a relief last night to be able to set things aside for a while, but now a new day was about to come up with the sun and problems had to be faced.

From the kitchen window she saw the dugout door open. Matt stepped out carrying a lantern in his fist with a shirt draped over his elbow.

The lantern swung with his stride, setting a circle of light swaying over the ground from the dugout to the pump in the yard.

Cruel was having to watch the man she could nearly taste on her tongue splashing water over his bare chest.

Cruel was watching him dip his hand into the bucket he had hauled up, with chest muscles pulling and stretching in the glow of the lamp. It was watching while he dumped water over his head, then shook his shoulder-kissing hair into the still inky dawn.

Cruel was asking her to leave the only home that had ever truly been hers. Making a choice like that would rip her heart in two. The very thought of it made her stomach queasy. She cared about Matt, more deeply than she had ever cared for anyone, but her four walls were her dream come true.

Without a doubt, between the two of them, Matt was the cruel one.

Emma dropped a dab of grease into the frying pan heating on the stove. She watched it pop and turn clear, spreading thinly over the black bottom of the skillet.

It might be only days until he left. She would have to hurry and make the new dress she had promised Lucy.

Or take her good time. But that would make her selfish. With death riding into town, Matt would have to go, and soon.

With a full day of chores stretched out before him, Matt stepped out of the dugout. The moon had set but stars still dotted the dark sky—the same ones that had twinkled on Emma's bare skin the whole night long.

A coyote howled far out beyond the creek. Matt's boots crunched the dried-out earth when he walked toward the well, but other than that, all the world slept, silent and still.

All the world but Emma, that is. He watched her

through the window while he approached the well. She still had on her party dress and hadn't yet done up her hair. Even from this distance he could see a sprig or two of grass wedged in with the curls.

She had to be mad as a pistol at him for asking her, again, to give up the thing most important to her.

Watching her move about the kitchen, turning something over in the skillet and stir something else, made his heart trip up inside him.

This was the woman most men only dreamed of. What man in town wouldn't give his best boots to be able to stand here in the dark and watch while she opened the oven door and slid in something to be baked?

Which one of them wouldn't give half a lifetime to be offered her body? Was he ten times over a fool not to take what she clearly wanted to give?

Matt lowered the bucket into the well and drew it up again full of fresh, morning-crisp water. He dumped some over his head, then shook it to clear out the image of Emma lying chaste but naked beside him.

He'd longed to taste her flesh when the moon had spun its magic on it. And now, again, when the heat from the stove blushed her cheeks pink.

Matt shrugged on his shirt, then tied his bandanna around his neck. He'd better feed the horses before his thoughts got the best of him. In another second he might find himself bursting through the kitchen door to take his wife right there on the table that she was cleaning with a soapy cloth.

If he had half as much sense as Red, which wasn't much these days, he'd say goodbye tomorrow. The house was finished and there was no longer anything to hold him here.

He ought to give her a long, hard kiss farewell first thing after chores. He'd do it for sure, if Emma hadn't promised to make Lucy a new dress.

"Mama Emma, when will you make my new dress?"

Emma lifted Lucy to the seat of the wagon, then checked to make sure Red had loaded the large bucket and the small one in the back along with four barrels of water.

"Not today. It might take most of the afternoon to get the trees watered."

It had been ten hot days since the last rain. If she didn't make the effort to water the saplings by hand they would dry out more quickly than the petticoat pinned on the clothesline.

As far as she could see, the sky stretched away with as pure a blue as she'd ever seen. The appearance of a big black cloud would be welcome. How many hours of work wouldn't a good downpour save?

"Well, then." Emma gathered up her skirt in one hand and grabbed hold of the wagon's wooden seat with the other to pull herself up. "I suppose new Mr. Hoppety Tree is ready for a good long drink, don't you?"

"Maybe after that he'll grow an apple."

"A big fat red one," Emma pronounced cheerfully to cover the sorrow that nipped at her heart knowing that Lucy wouldn't be here to eat that apple.

Emma clicked to the team. They turned toward the barn door, then set out at a slow pace toward the grove of tender young trees.

"Step carefully, ladies. We don't want to overturn the water."

"Do horsies know words?"

"Maybe one or two."

"Fluffy and Princess know lots of words."

"They don't know *stay outside*," Emma pointed out.

Lucy sighed and spread her palms. "They know it—they just don't like it."

Emma touched Lucy's chin and lifted her face. "It's your job to make them like it."

"Just like you make me like to wear a bonnet?"

Hopefully, Lucy would have more luck. Emma tugged and straightened the pink bow under the child's chin. "Yes, something like that."

"They won't—oh! Mama Emma, look!" Lucy bounced up and pointed her finger at a fat red cow. "A cow got inside the fence!"

Cut again! Lands, Lawrence Pendragon was a persistent man. Did he think he could wear her down with a snip of wire?

At least only one cow had gotten through and hadn't noticed yet how sweet and green the young trees were.

"Wait here in the wagon, baby, while I shoo the pesky thing away."

With each step she took, parched grass cracked underfoot. Far off, the baked horizon shimmered in waves of dry heat.

Luckily the bovine didn't need more than a well-placed whack with a shovel on its rump to set it scurrying for the open range.

Emma lifted Lucy from the front of the wagon, then set her down in the back.

"Take the little bucket and fill up the big one for me," she said. "We'd better get this finished soon so that Papa or Uncle Billy can come back and mend the fence before supper."

"Okay, Mama." Lucy filled her bucket three times, dumping it into the big one.

Emma lifted the large pail with both hands. The weight of it cut the iron handle into her palm. After watering only five trees, her dress had begun to stick to her sweating skin.

Red welts chafed the creases of her palms. She'd have to hide them from Matt since he'd use her aching hands as proof that she needed a husband to take care of the heavy work.

All she really needed was to remember to bring along Matt's big leather gloves.

"Can my new dress be blue?"

"Blue with flowers, or pure blue?" she called over her shoulder, nearly breathless as she dumped the water into the dirt well ringing a sapling.

A hired man to work the place might be a good idea, although he'd probably expect to be fed on a daily basis. A husband, even a hungry one, wouldn't require a salary.

"Blast," she muttered under her breath. She wouldn't come around to that way of thinking, no matter how much less it would cost. At least a hired man could be let go when she didn't need him anymore, and he wouldn't expect to sleep in the house.

"Blue with apples."

It might take some time to find blue apple fabric. The thought snuck up from the back of her mind and pleased her before she had a chance to think better of it.

Precious time that she could use to adjust to Matt's leaving. She could use it to soak up the sight of him sitting tall on Thunder's back, the way he did early each morning, looking out over the homestead as if he was judging what kind of day it might be. Most times he turned to look at her standing on the porch with a grin shining on his face.

Matt loved this life. It showed in his smile and the flash of sudden humor that came to him all at once for no reason that she could think of. Any time of day she heard it in his song, whether he sang to the horses or the nail he was hammering into a fence.

If she took each stitch of Lucy's dress nice and slowly she would have time to dream about what it would be like if he came to her in the night.

Precious time, but dangerous.

Each moment that Matt delayed his departure brought Hawker closer. And delay was far too easy.

It had been his idea, a week back with Lucy sitting on his lap, rocking beside the fireplace while Emma mended his shirt, that she should sew the child a new dress before the trip to San Francisco.

She'd been to town since then, twice, and each time she'd "forgotten" to purchase the fabric for the dress. Maybe it was because the sewing of that dress was the last promise to be kept. It was the only thing holding Matt here.

What foolishness. They both knew the dress was an excuse. She was the one holding Matt here. She and the home they were building...together.

She could see him now far in the distance, clearing the firebreak with Billy.

Emma closed her eyes and tried to picture a new house in San Francisco. She had never lived in a big city; neither had Matt. Maybe she ought to consider it. If she agreed to go, they might all be safe...and homesick.

More foolishness! Her roots were here, deep in her own soil.

Fanciful feelings aside, she wanted him to go...truly. It had been her plan all along—they'd agreed to it.

With half a breath of encouragement, and a kiss for luck, Matt would stay and take his chances with Hawker. He'd made that clear on the night of the party, but she would end up as dead as Matt with the guilt of his murder on her heart.

Emma brought the bucket back for Lucy to fill again.

"After the noon meal tomorrow, I'll go find you some blue apple fabric."

This would be the quickest dress she'd ever made. The times were precious and dangerous—she couldn't do a thing to change that. But she wouldn't make them selfish times.

To keep Matt from staying beyond what was safe she'd sew until her fingers grew raw.

Chapter Ten

Emma glanced up from a blue-checkered bolt of fabric to see the young shopkeeper at Rath and Wright's staring at her.

His gaze slid away as though he had caught her doing something embarrassing.

She would have liked to think that his behavior was odd, but no less than six others had given her the same look. From Lulu Frolic hanging feather-clad over the balcony of Mollie's Palace to the prim Harold Goodhew herding his group of students up the schoolhouse steps, those half-lidded glances had been the same.

Had some scorching rumor been started over Woody Vance's attention toward her? In a town like Dodge where life was lived to its most colorful, a common flirtation hardly seemed remarkable.

Emma gave her full attention to the display of cotton fabric set before her. As she had suspected, there was not a combination of blue and apples. The blue check would be sweet, though, and she could embroider the apples around the collar.

Emma carried the blue-checkered bolt to the counter. She'd buy plenty so that Lucy could grow a bit in it.

"I'd like a package of that red embroidery thread behind the counter, too."

"Yes, ma'am." The clerk cut the fabric, folded it in a neat bundle, then placed the red thread on top.

During the transaction he'd gone from staring at his hands to watching out the window as though a new customer were about to come through the door with a wheelbarrow full of money to spend.

Strange that he seemed to look everywhere but in her eyes.

"You have a fine day, Efran," she said, turning toward the door.

"Yes, ma'am…you, too, Mrs. Suede."

The young clerk was certainly fidgety about something, but chances were it had nothing to do with her. She'd never been the kind of person to draw much attention and very likely those odd glances were just that… odd.

Outside on the boardwalk, the wind picked up her skirts and snapped them against her calves. A horse tethered at the hitching post sneezed at the dust stirred up from the street. It shook its mane and pawed the ground.

Apparently the animal didn't like the low moan of the wind racing around the eaves of the porch. The poor beast seemed as tense as the store clerk.

It was certainly an odd day in Dodge. Thank goodness Pearl was boarded at Jesse's livery for the afternoon where she wouldn't pick up on the feeling that something was not quite right.

Emma tightened the bonnet straps under her chin

when the wind bucked against it. She clutched the goods for Lucy's dress to her chest and leaned into the gust.

If only it would rain. Everything felt dried out. A body could practically hear the ground cracking and crying out for moisture. And her skin! What wouldn't she give to fill her lovely bathtub with butter and cream and soak the afternoon away?

The indulgent thought nearly made her laugh out loud. The afternoon was slipping away as it was. As soon as she delivered a bottle of Orange Lilly to Rachael Sizeloff it was off to home and preparing a bit of supper for the men and Lucy.

Bathing in buttermilk, indeed! If the thought was wayward, the picture that popped into her brain and slowed her steps was positively wicked. Wouldn't Matt be distressed if he could see the two of them in her mind, rolling about in the tub wearing nothing but cream?

From a block away, she spotted Joseph Sizeloff sweeping the steps of the church. His vest slapped against his shirt in the wind and Emma wondered why he bothered with sweeping when what dirt he managed to clear away was immediately blown back in place.

"Good afternoon, Mr. Sizeloff. Is Rachael inside?" Emma was forced to shout over the deviltry that swirled from every direction at once. "I've got her Orange Lilly."

"You missed her by ten minutes. Little Maudie needed a nap and she's got to prepare the sermon for Sunday." He set the broom against the rail of the church porch, but it blew over with a clatter and scrape. "Come on inside for a minute and get out of this wind. There's fresh coffee on the stove."

"I'm off for home, but I could do with a cup before I head back, thank you."

Before she set foot on the third step, Joseph Sizeloff's smile sagged under his mustache. He gazed past the top of her head, looking at the stretch of prairie with a frown.

Stepping onto the highest stair of the porch, she smelled the trouble that Joseph had spotted so far off.

Smoke! It tickled her nose, then blew away with the next gust of wind.

"Prairie fire," he murmured.

Emma stretched up on her toes trying to spot the flames, but all she saw was black smoke coming up from the ground, like a thundercloud settled to earth.

"I'll have to pass on the coffee." Emma turned to dash down the steps. "I've got to get home before the fire cuts off the road."

"Hold on there, Mrs. Suede." He caught her elbow. "It's best you stay with Rachael and me tonight. With the way the wind's pushing the fire, you'd never make it. By morning it will have moved on and the ground cooled enough for your horse to get you safely home."

"But I have to get there now. What if my house burns down?" By the second, the smoke grew blacker. It billowed higher in the sky and the scent of it no longer blew away. "If anything happens they'll need me."

"From the direction that the wind is blowing now, it ought to cut right between your place and town. Your house should be safe enough. Wait just a minute while I bank the stove inside, and I'll walk you back to our place."

"I hate to put you out."

"You won't be in the way. Rachael will be glad to have a new ear to practice Sunday's sermon on."

"Well, then, I'd be pleased to stay with your family this evening, but there's no need to leave before you intended. I know the way and I need to make a stop at the livery to let Jesse know that Pearl will be staying the night."

"All right, then. Tell my wife I'll be along in about an hour."

By the time Emma had bid Joseph Sizeloff goodbye and walked halfway to the livery, ash had begun to filter from the sky like dirty snowflakes.

A woman came out of the bakery and looked up at the sky with her apron held over her nose and mouth. A big red dog leaped out of a wagon hitched in front of the bank. It ran in circles barking and making the horses nervous. A man dashed outside and opened his mouth to scold the dog, but when he saw the ash coming down he whistled and motioned for the dog to get back aboard. He jumped up on his wagon and urged his team out of town at a lumber-creaking pace.

All up and down the street windows slammed closed and doors banged shut. The slap of wood on wood and the nervous call of voices echoed over town.

Near the railroad, cattle bawled in the stock pens. The poor beasts didn't know that a wide firebreak had been maintained all around the town. Even if the flames came close enough for Dodge to be in danger of flying embers, folks would be on the lookout. Already the baker had set out four pails of water on the boardwalk.

The town wasn't likely to catch fire. From what Emma could see, the flames were miles outside town.

It was only the wind blowing in the smoke and ash that made the danger seem so immediate.

Surely Rachael's husband had been right about the fire not burning her home. She would make herself believe it and not go running through a blazing prairie fire thinking she could save the place. As much as she loved her home, she wouldn't risk her safety and that of Pearl to watch it incinerate before her eyes.

Matt, Billy and Red had been diligent about keeping the firebreak cleared. Emma snuffed out her worry. She tucked it in the back of her mind and looked forward to an evening with Rachael's family. Certainly, tomorrow morning she would find her home as intact as she had left it today.

An acrid wind whistled down the street and pushed Emma's bonnet into her eyes.

"Blast!" She shoved it back with the fingers of one hand and gripped her fabric tight to her chest with the other. "Cursed wind!"

If only there had been room in her purse for the Orange Lilly as well as the material, her progress toward the livery would have been quicker. As it was, she had to stop every third step to pull the dratted bonnet into place. If it hadn't been for the ash so thick in the air she would have let it flap behind her.

All at once the perverse wind seemed to lose interest in her bonnet and tossed up her skirt instead. It flew up about her petticoats. When she tried to press it modestly down a gust caught the fabric for Lucy's dress and spun it right out of her clenched fingers.

It looked like a blue-checkered tumbleweed racing across the street toward the Long Branch.

"Oh blazes!" she cried, and took off after it at a run.

Her petticoats flashed white to the knee but she didn't care. Imagine having to wash perfectly new material before it could be sewn!

The checkered fabric came to rest, wrapped around the thick thighs of a man standing outside the saloon.

Emma stopped short. She stood in the middle of the street with her hair streaking out of its bun as if it was possessed.

Daylight borrowing an unnatural orange tint from the sun had settled down on the town. It made the scene before her appear absurd. Even though the stranger looked intimidating, like a big mean bull trapped on the boardwalk, she covered her mouth to keep from giggling while he struggled to untangle the creeping fabric from his legs. The harder he plucked at it the more wrapped up he became in its checkered claws.

Apparently the wind was not satisfied with tormenting him with a gingham skirt. It took a sudden updraft and knocked the hat from his shaved head. His hand shot out. Nearly as fast as Emma could see it, he caught the hat by its black brim and smashed it back on his head.

The wind sighed softly all of a sudden, giving him an instant to free himself of the fabric, then fold it neatly from corner to corner then side to side.

"Ma'am?" He held her wayward goods out to her with long slender fingers that didn't match his stocky frame. One shiny fingernail caught the orange glow of the sky. What an odd day when a man's fingers looked like flaming matches.

Under any other circumstances she would not have approached a stranger standing in front of the saloon.

Mercy, but wouldn't Matt and the boys have something to say about her meeting this crooked-nosed stranger without them beside her.

Why, they would raise dust from here to home to see her coming up the saloon steps with no more sense than the dry leaves blowing wild in the street. Still, she had paid good money for that fabric and she wouldn't shy away just because the fellow had silver eyes that peeked out of lashless slits in his face, or just because they looked as if they might shoot out bullets more easily than goodwill.

She wouldn't cower in the street because the man had been conversing with Gray Derby Bart when her purchase had taken to the wind.

She plastered her most fetching smile on her lips and ignored Bart's I'd-like-to-drown-a-puppy glare at her. With the other man present she was likely to be safe from the scoundrel.

"Thank you for rescuing my property." She plucked the fabric from his narrow fingers, then took a step back. "I'm sorry it caused you so much trouble."

"No trouble at all, ma'am." His voice rumbled like black coal in his chest, but he shot her a crooked smile that met the eastward slant of his nose. The gesture looked like a half-moon shining on his face and he didn't look so intimidating.

Bart, stretching up in his boots, whispered in the man's ear.

"Well, good day," she said. The three steps from the boardwalk to the street felt like twenty. The bald man didn't seem so sinister now that he had smiled, but Bart looked as if he had drowned the pups and was now on the prowl for kittens.

"I'm sorry for your loss, Mrs. Suede," the deep voice said.

"I beg your pardon?" Emma turned. The wind raced about her head and the orange air prickled the hair on her arms. Her stomach felt as if that long-fingered hand had reached inside her and twisted it.

"You could beg, but it won't do no good." Bart's rheumy eyes glistened and his tongue, coated white, darted out to lick his lips. "This here is Angus Hawker, come all the way from prison to shoot your man dead."

"No harm meant to you, missus, but there's a score to be evened."

He tipped his hat; the half-moon smile sagged to a quarter before he walked back into the Long Branch.

"Whoo-eee!" Bart slapped his derby on his knee. "Don't you worry any, sweet thing, old Bart will come courting before week's end. Your bed won't even have time to cool off."

Ordinarily singing made a chore move along more smoothly. Nails were hammered into wood straighter and a heavy load felt lighter. But Matt didn't sing while he swept out Pearl's stall. He listened. In a quiet corner Lucy hummed to her little dogs. He couldn't see her over the stall sides, but her voice rose through the dust twirling in the beam of light that slashed through the open barn doors. It pleased him to know that he had handed on the gift to her. It would help her through the sorry times.

The shifting of fresh hay through the pitchfork drowned out the rest of her tune, but Matt tucked the memory of it away in his heart, saving the sound for a time when the voice would be grown.

Would she always sing from her heart, like a pretty yellow lark fluttering over the land?

So far, life hadn't given her sadness, just days full of laughing in the sunshine, playing with pups and being the darling of all.

Matt filled Pearl's trough with hay. The horse would nuzzle his ribs when she returned from Dodge. She was an unusual animal, more of a pet than livestock. Her blindness was no handicap—it seemed only to make her more perceptive.

"Good old Pearl," he muttered, hanging the pitchfork on a nail hammered into the barn wall.

Matt walked toward the trill of Lucy's voice. He found her lying in the pile of straw outside Thunder's stall.

"You look as sweet as sunshine singing to your pups, baby girl, but I've got to put this straw in Thunder's stall."

Lucy stood and stretched. "Papa, bend down. You have hay in your hair."

Matt stooped low and let her take it out.

"When's Mama Emma coming home?"

"I'm sure she's on her way right now."

"I'm glad." Having plucked out the last bit of hay, Lucy fluffed his hair about his ears. "Will she make my new dress tonight?"

Probably, but he hoped not. As soon as it was sewn, he'd have no excuse to put off his departure.

Still, it was past time he had a talk with his daughter about going to California, but how did a man find the words to break a little girl's heart?

"Come on, sunshine baby, let's go to the kitchen and have some of those oatmeal cookies that Emma left for us. Maybe by the time we've finished, she'll be home."

"Carry me, Papa."

"Those little legs of yours run out of steps already?"

Lucy giggled and wrapped her arms about his neck when he lifted her.

"Legs don't run out of steps, silly papa—they're just resting."

Inside the kitchen, Matt plopped Lucy down on a chair at the table. He hoped the plate of cookies he set between them would ease the thing he was about to tell her.

"I got a letter from your grandma in San Francisco." Matt sucked in a deep breath and wished he were singing.

Lucy took a bite of her cookie, then put it down. She chewed slowly and swallowed.

"You've heard me mention Grandma Suede?"

"Yes, she has a pretty house on a hill with a big glass window so you can see the Pacific Ocean."

"How would you like to take a long train ride all the way to California to see her?"

"I'd like it, Papa." Lucy picked up her cookie but set it down without taking a bite. "But Fluffy and Princess would bark at everybody."

Lordy, even a song wouldn't make what he had to tell her any easier.

"Finish up that cookie," he said, stalling.

"I'm not hungry."

"Not hungry? You love Emma's cookies, darlin'. Eat as many as you like."

Lucy took one more bite, then lost interest in the treat.

"We'd have to leave the dogs here." How could words feel like a razor slicing up a man's throat?

"But if you and me and Mama Emma and Red and

Billy go on the train, who will take care of Fluffy and Princess? Pearl will get real lonely."

While he wrestled with the words to break his child's heart, he heard hoofbeats pounding fast, racing past the well and pulling up outside the front door.

Two pairs of boots slammed against the front porch, coming around to the kitchen door.

The door flew open and hit the wall. Good thing Emma wasn't home yet. She'd have boxed Red's and Billy's ears for sure for treating her house so.

"Fire!" Winded, Red slipped into a chair. He spotted the cookies and ate one whole.

"Cutting straight between here and Dodge," Billy added.

"Faster than a son of a gun." Red spoke through the crumbs in his mouth.

Matt felt the blood drain from his face, and his fingers turned cold even though the kitchen was warm.

Surely Emma would see the fire and have the sense to stay in Dodge. Common intelligence would keep her where it was safe. She wouldn't come flying home thinking that she could save her home if the fire turned this way.

Anyone would have the sense to stay put.

"Damn!" he shouted. Too late, he noticed Lucy's eyes go round in surprise.

He bolted for the corral where Thunder lifted his inky nose to the sky, sniffing the air.

A farmer racing toward town on his big plow horse waved his hat at Emma.

"Go back!" She saw his lips move but she couldn't

hear him. She sat atop Pearl's back with the wind howling around her head and her heart hammering in her ears.

Already she'd gotten the same advice from a family rushing for the safety of town in their wagon, countless jackrabbits and several deer.

If Emma hadn't listened to them, she wouldn't listen to the farmer's ever-so-wise advice, either.

Good Pearl turned her nose toward a pack of prairie wolves who had stopped a hundred feet to the west to give the horse a look that said if the day were different they would have her for a snack. Pearl snorted but didn't shy from the threat. The canines, with the sense that the good Lord had given them, trotted away from the threat of the oncoming flames.

Emma had sent her good sense packing since Angus Hawker had come to town. Those fingers, so quick they could catch a hat right out of the wind, put more fear in her heart than any distant, if quickly approaching, fire.

As soon as the flames burned out she would make sure Matt and his family boarded the train out of Dodge. Somehow, some way that she couldn't think of right now, Hawker wouldn't know they were at the train station.

She'd find a way to make everyone think he was working hard on the homestead when all the while he was halfway to the West Coast.

Ideas scurried willy-nilly in her brain but wouldn't settle into a logical plan any more than the frantic quail underfoot could form an orderly line to flee from the fire. The ground seemed to be alive with birds running in circles, as though they had forgotten they could fly.

She felt like a swimmer going against a tide of squirrels, deer, rabbits and every other creature with more sense than she had.

"Come on, Pearl, we've got to go faster. Matt's bound to come looking for us." The horse, while not unwilling to follow the road home, went at her own cautious pace.

"Hawker will kill Matt if he goes into town."

Pearl stopped to snort when a wisp of smoke curled over the road and across her hooves.

"Come on, girl, that fire is moving a whole lot faster than we are."

The horse tested the road, one careful footfall at a time. Apparently she expected to step on hot coals at any moment.

After only a quarter of a mile, she stopped altogether. Maybe Pearl's eyes had begun to burn like Emma's had.

Lordy, it felt as though she stood on the windward side of a campfire. Her hair became saturated with the scent of burning prairie grass, and her throat felt raw and dry.

No more than a mile down the road the air looked clear and breathable. If only she could convince Pearl to move, they could be on their way and catch Matt before he rode blindly into horrible danger.

And ride he would. Hadn't he already faced the preacher for her? Hadn't he ridden into a storm, with crazed cattle on the verge of mayhem, to pluck her right out of the muck? Could she ever forget how he'd knelt, bare chested beside her in the mud and the rain, braving who knew what kind of fever or illness, to help save her trees?

Emma had no doubt that Matt would ride right into the sights of Angus Hawker's gun to see her safe from the fire without knowing his danger.

"He'd come even if he knew, wouldn't he, Pearl? He'd come with Hawker's gun pointed right at his heart to see us safe."

From high on Pearl's back, Emma watched the flames' orange teeth eating up the grass. From this distance they looked no more than knee-high. She could probably jump right over the fiery line if she held her skirts high enough. There was still time to get to safety if only she could convince the horse to move.

"Get along, Pearl." She clucked her tongue, but the only movement from the horse was a shiver running from the tip of her nose to the flick of her tail.

Emma slid off her back. "I know it's frightening, not being able to see the danger. But we're going home."

Emma tugged gently on Pearl's reins and urged her down the road. The smoke grew suddenly thicker and the clear spot up ahead farther away.

On the far side of the smoke, dust kicked up from the road some distance off. Relief swept through her at the thought it might be Matt. She'd catch him before he went galloping into town.

After a few moments she heard the creek of a buggy and the hoofbeats of a pair of horses, coming fast. She pulled Pearl to the side of the road when she thought the driver might not see them, coming through the haze as fast as he was.

The buggy, carrying a man and a young woman, rattled by and kicked up enough dust to make her cough. It mixed with the smoke and took its time settling back to the ground. Through the haze she recognized the reckless driver.

Of course the man would assume the road belonged to him alone.

Blast! Lawrence Pendragon had reined in his team and turned the buggy around. How ridiculous he looked, puffing on his infernal cigarette when the whole countryside was being incinerated!

"Have you lost your way, Mrs. Suede?" Pendragon plucked the smoldering stub from his lips.

"Certainly not."

"You can't mean to continue on this road." He leaned forward in his seat. "The fire will cut you off from front and back. You'll never make it."

Mercy, but she wasn't about to explain her need to get home and warn Matt about Angus Hawker. Pendragon would like nothing more than to see her a helpless widow.

"In that case I'd better hurry along my way," she said.

"Don't be a little fool. Turn back."

A fool? A little fool!

"Why you low-down…" Lenore moved closer to her father, making room for Emma. "Your cowboys probably started this fire!"

Lawrence Pendragon leaned across his daughter to speak. "That may be, but not by my orders, and not intentionally. My cattle graze this land."

Lenore tugged at her father's sleeve, looking paler by the second. "Papa, make Mrs. Suede get in the wagon and come along with us!" Lenore reached her hand toward Emma.

"You'll never make it."

Oh, she would make it. More than her own life depended on it.

She pulled on Pearl's reins, hoping the horse didn't dig her hooves into the dirt in stubborn defiance, or worse yet, take it into her mind to follow the wagon.

"I'd have more luck getting my prize bull to get up in this wagon and swear off cows," Pendragon answered.

At last he had said something she agreed with. Her shoes would have to be sparking flames before she would accept his help.

He snapped a whip at the horse's ear to set his team racing down the road toward town. Lenore clung to the side of the buggy, looking back at her.

A glance north told Emma that her shoes would indeed be sparking flames if Pearl didn't get moving.

Chapter Eleven

Matt couldn't tell which pounded harder, Thunder's hooves tearing up clods of prairie sod in the mad rush toward Dodge, or his heart slamming against his ribs for fear that Emma had been caught on the road with the fire closing in.

If she believed her precious house would burn, a dozen folks talking good sense wouldn't make her stay put.

Grit and backbone were a pair of qualities that Matt loved best in his wife. Unfortunately, when her house was involved, those good traits came smack up against a lack of common sense and it made his insides feel like a nervous herd of beeves.

"Dear God," Matt whispered. Bending low over Thunder's neck, he rode loose and let the stallion stretch out to his quickest stride. "Make her stay in town… damn it, Emma, stay in town!"

She wouldn't know how fast a prairie fire could spread. It might seem a mile away one minute and the next have a person boxed in. She wouldn't know how the smoke could kill you before you ever saw the flames.

Stay in town, darlin', stay in town.

The fire spread from north to south, a blazing arrow headed straight for the road to Dodge. If he could get past the point where the fire would cross over, he'd be able to get to Emma. He'd take her to the boardinghouse and sit on her all day and night if that's what it took to keep her in a sensible place.

A wolf raced past Thunder, but neither of the animals took the time to threaten or fear each other. The wolf was as bent on his survival as Matt and Thunder were on Emma's.

The sky turned from crystal-blue to ominous orange in a matter of seconds and wind shot ash, but Thunder didn't miss a step. His bold hooves kept pounding the ground.

Stay in town...stay in town, stay safe...stay safe.

He slipped his bandanna up, protecting his nose and mouth from the grit that snowed out of the sky. Without a doubt, Thunder breathed in more soot than he ought to. The brave horse, clearly sensing Matt's urgency, ran without hesitation toward the danger that every other creature had the good sense to flee from.

Matt closed his eyes against a sudden gust of cinders. Thunder slowed, then stopped. The stallion paced in a nervous circle for a moment before he turned south, bolting away from the road.

"Back to the road!" Thunder ignored the tug on his reins and Matt's shout. He stretched his long neck and ran. Land fell away beneath his hooves in a blur. Who could blame the animal for seeking the safety of the river? It was instinct to want to stay alive. He prayed that Emma had listened to that instinct.

After a moment of cursing his mount's sudden stubbornness, he heard a panicked whicker. It hadn't come from Thunder.

Just ahead, Pearl pranced in a circle. Beyond her a wicked pall of smoke smothered the land. She pawed up clods of dry grass and neighed in fright.

Racing forward, Thunder answered, his call no less agitated. Pearl lifted her nose, sniffed, then dashed into the deadly cloud.

Within seconds Thunder followed. Matt felt blinded. The air had grown too hot and thick to breathe.

Pearl would never be out here by herself. She would never have dashed into this hell of heat and blinding soot if Emma hadn't been inside. He could only pray that with their clearly better instincts, the horses would find her.

Thunder stopped and pawed the ground. Pearl snorted. Lying near their hooves under a swirl of suffocating smoke lay Emma with her face in the dirt and her hair tangled across her back reflecting the red glow of approaching flames.

Matt dropped from Thunder's back. The descent seemed like a fall from a cliff. Heat blistered his face. His clothes felt as if they were being pressed by a hot iron on laundry day with him still in them.

"Emma!" Her name ripped out of his throat, scalding as though the flames had gotten inside him.

So faint that he barely heard it, she murmured, "Pearl."

"Get up, darlin'. We've got to get where we can breathe." More murmuring, mostly nonsense, trembled against his ear.

A fit of coughing shook Matt. A nest of hornets buzzing in his chest would have felt better. Without fresh air he wasn't sure that he could lift Emma onto Thunder's back. He scooped his arms beneath her and managed to stand, but he still had another foot to lift.

"Come down, boy."

The good horse, going against every instinct that would be natural to him, dipped closer to them.

Emma was a little thing and it shouldn't have winded him to set her on Thunder's back, but the strength had been robbed from his muscles.

It felt like a duel with gravity just to climb behind her. He coughed the order for Thunder to get going. Luckily the stallion understood the need without having to be told in clear words.

Matt prayed that the horse would get clear of danger before he, too, felt weak from the effects of the strangling air. Trusting Thunder to do what needed doing, Matt braced his thighs about the horse.

Run like hell, boy, he thought when the words would not shoot past his raw throat.

Let's go, Pearl, he said in his mind, but when he looked back she was gone. He thought he heard an equine cry in the distance, but he couldn't be sure.

In only a minute, the air grew clearer. Roaring flames became a distant crackle. Thunder didn't slow to a trot until the only sound whistling about their heads was the natural wind.

"That's good." Matt's voice! Sounding raw…coughing.

"Take a deep breath, darlin'." Calloused fingers stroked her throat. A stone cut into her back. Fingers pressed her breastbone and then her ribs. "One more time, Emma, breathe!"

She coughed and tasted smoke and charred soot. With a long gasp her body filled with clean prairie air. Breath after deep breath filled her lungs.

Gradually the unnatural lethargy that had overcome her mind cleared. Her gaze focused on his eyes, simmering amber and worried. But relieved, too.

She hadn't died after all.

"Matt?" His breathing seemed as labored as hers. With a groan that stretched to heaven and back, he snatched her up, freeing her of the pebble biting her back. He rocked her against his chest, so that his mad heartbeat was like her own.

He held her the way Lucy held her rag doll, tender but possessive. Since a rag doll is what she felt like, she relaxed into the embrace, listening to the rush of Matt's breath near her ear.

"You scared the hell out of me. I thought I'd lost you for sure." His arms, tight with tension, braced her. Sanctuary in a world spun out of control.

At last he set her away at arm's length with his steadying hands gripping her elbows. With a quick glance he checked her over from head to boot toe.

How cruel fate was, to bring her this man out of the blue, get her to love him until she couldn't think straight and then force her to send him away. Her heart was breaking into sharp slivers of regret for what would never be.

Matt had the look of a man redeemed, so thankful that he hadn't lost her.

But he had lost her. And she had lost him. In only a few hours he and his family would be on the train out of Dodge. How did a body find the strength to face it?

It didn't have to be this way, though. He had given

her a choice. Leaving her land could not be any more heart-wrenching than this. Didn't the sun rise in Matt's smile as well as over her land?

She pushed away from him, aching over the parting to come. Knowing that she had a choice, that she could prevent it by giving up her home, only made the pain worse.

"Get up, Matt." She tried to stand but couldn't, yet. Matt helped her up and brushed soot from her ruined skirt. "There's no time for that now. Hawker's here, in Dodge."

"So you came to warn me?"

"You can't think I would be out here for any other reason."

She took one step toward Thunder with Matt holding her arm. She gazed over the land, burning like a fury in one direction and clear as paradise the other. Small hairs prickled along her neck.

She turned as though in slow motion; her body felt heavy, cold with dread. Her hands flew to her mouth. "Matt, where's Pearl?"

Red shoved his hands into his pockets and kicked a dirt clod with a flick of his boot. Standing beside the corral fence, with his wild hair blazing against the setting sun, the boy looked as ill-tempered as a bull stung on his tender parts.

"You can't make me leave here." Red stomped another clod, pounding it to dust. "I could take down Hawker blindfolded and turned backward."

"When your brain begins to grow as fast as your body, son, you'll know how foolish that sounds." Matt would give up a lot to be able to stay here, too. It hadn't seemed so long ago that he had behaved in the same way as Red was now. His mother had looked hurt and deeply worried when he had dug in his heels and refused to relocate to California. Moving away would hurt more now than it would have then, and if it weren't for those who depended on him, he wouldn't do it.

To take a piece of barren ground, mix it up with some sweat and lumber, and turn it into a home was a satisfaction that he hadn't expected. Watching sunrise then sunset on this land, day after day, put a bone-deep longing in him to stay and let his roots grow deep.

With Emma the heartbeat of the homestead, it was going to be nearly impossible to say goodbye. He wasn't certain that he would be strong enough to do it.

And didn't Emma depend on him as well as the children? It might be that leaving was as wrong as staying.

The last of the sun's rays turned the smoke from the distant fire a deep ruby color. Before daylight, if the wind didn't shift, the blaze would reach the river and burn itself out.

"Least I know better than to run away and leave Emma out here alone. A man has a duty by a woman, to keep her safe from the world," Red said.

"What you know about women wouldn't fill a water pail. Hell, I don't know much more than that even with my extra years."

The scarlet glow in Red's hair dulled to russet when the sun dipped below the horizon. Sundown wind pricked the grass and made it whisper around their boots and across the homestead.

"It's cowardly to run. If you're too scared to face Hawker, I'll do it myself."

Matt reached over and gripped Red's shoulder. He

gave it a firm squeeze. The boy looked away, gazing across the prairie.

He understood Red's feelings. It hadn't been so long ago that Matt had been a young hothead. Even now, appearing cowardly would be hard as hell. Out here, cowardice was only one sin above murder.

If he did face Hawker, though, it would not be out of vanity. Keeping his family safe was the only choice to be considered. As much as he wanted to hang on to both his pride and his life, if it came down to it he would make either sacrifice.

"I'll admit that you're too big to be tied in the barn like an ignorant colt, but I'll do it if it means keeping you from getting shot. Don't think you can beat Hawker, son. You'd never get your gun clear of the leather. The fact that you've never killed a man before and he's laid a score of them in the ground should say all you need to know."

Red shook his shoulder free of Matt's grip.

"I'm fast! You don't know how fast I am!"

"It wouldn't matter how fast you are. You're decent inside. If you were to face that killer, there would be a second where you would think about the life you were taking. In that one hair of an instant, he'd have you."

"You can't make me go someplace I don't want to go and you can't keep me from going to town neither."

Low on the eastern horizon, a few stars popped against the sky. Soon they'd take their dance across the night. Those glorious sparkling steps never faltered. He'd watched them slide by on his nights sleeping on the trail, always the same.

How could life go on so predictably above when

down here, in Kansas, it seemed to develop complications with each new wind?

"I suppose that's true. But here's the thing about being a man that you need to learn. Your actions have consequences to the folks who care about you. You've got to consider how Emma and Lucy would feel seeing you lowered into the ground up at Boot Hill. And don't be such a fool to think they wouldn't see it."

Red sagged against the corral fence. He freed his hands from his pockets and relaxed his balled-up fists.

Matt leaned into the fence, shoulder to shoulder with Red.

"You see Emma over there rocking on the porch and staring out toward Dodge?"

"She's been sitting there like that ever since you brought her home half smoked," Red said.

"If she feels such grief over a horse, think of what she would feel for you."

"Pearl was a good old blind horse." Red tried to smooth his hair with the palm of his hand, but it stuck up through his fingers like prickly spikes of straw.

If the outside of the boy couldn't be tamed, what hope did Matt have of taming the inside?

The front door of the house opened. A beam of yellow light spilled over the porch and shone on Lucy climbing onto Emma's lap. She drew up her legs and tucked in her arms while Emma wrapped her up in arms full of motherly tenderness.

If it had been difficult telling Red to be ready to take the train out of town first thing in the morning, it would be pure hell breaking the news to Lucy.

"Maybe we ought to see if there's something we can

do about supper," Red said. "I don't think Emma's got the heart for it tonight."

Matt clapped Red on the shoulder. "Now you sound like a man. A good man."

It might take some doing to see that Red lived long enough to fulfill the promise of that good man he would be, but Matt would reach out from the grave to see it done if that's what it took.

After sundown the wind picked up and a chill crept over the prairie to announce the arrival of autumn.

Emma was beyond grateful to be sitting in her rocker beside the stone fireplace. Who would have thought that creeping cold would seep through the floor and up her legs when only hours ago heat had nearly killed her?

It took some nerve-settling to accept the friendly flicker of fire in her hearth as a blessing after living through a prairie fire. This one's lapping flames blushed heat against her face and tickled her toes with warmth. The other's rage had left her with a grieving heart. If it hadn't been for Matt, she would have perished along with dear Pearl.

How many times would that scene play over in her mind? Would it be days or weeks or even months before she would stop seeing that long prairie stretching away with only one horse nibbling at the dry grass?

She had sensed what had happened to Pearl before she ever found the voice to ask Matt. His words had come to her along with his arms, gentle but heavy with sorrow.

"It's a wonder that any of us made it out of there, darlin'." He'd looped one arm about her waist and tugged her back tight to his chest. "Pearl must have gotten confused with all the noise and smoke. She didn't follow us out of the fire."

At her first sob he'd turned her about and folded her up in both arms. He'd stroked her hair and whispered in her ear. He'd let her weep against his chest, first with great racking sobs of denial, then later with heart-wrenching moans of despair.

Not once did he mention his own life-threatening situation. If he had given a thought to Hawker in those moments he didn't say so and hadn't since. He'd kissed her hair, pressed her tight to his heart. When her grief turned to trembling, he'd scooped her up, settled her in front of him on Thunder's back and sung softly in her ear all the way home.

For the tenth time in an hour, Emma closed her eyes and listened for the clop of hooves outside the window. It might not be right to hold out vain hope—better to get on with the realities of life and accept them. Still, maybe Pearl had found a way out of the fire. She might come home. If Emma listened hard enough maybe the clipped gait of Pearl's trot would thump across the yard. She'd hear it easily over the pop and crackle of the lamb-like flames in the fireplace.

Outside, a coyote howled and got no returning cry. Silence stretched long. There was an unnatural stillness on the plains tonight. She pictured the poor beast rambling for miles and still not locating its pack.

From the bedroom she heard Matt whispering softly to Lucy. Quilts rustled and settled when he tucked her in. The smack of his lips whispered against her forehead.

It was a shame about the wolf. How many other creatures had been separated from all that was familiar? Dens and nests ruined, families shattered?

If tonight seemed so desolate, what would tomorrow night bring? With Matt gone, as he certainly would be, would she find herself in the barn keeping company with the pups?

Her house, her dream of dreams, with every comfort a woman could want, should be enough to see her through any despair. Its good solid walls would shut out misery and heartache.

Without a doubt, her home made every one of life's burdens lighter. Didn't it?

She glanced about her parlor. Her very own walls glowed amber in the lamplight and shut out the wind that whistled over and under the eaves, leaving her safe and warm. But were they more of a comfort than a husband's arms?

Footsteps clicked down the hall. The rocking chair across from her creaked with Matt settling into it.

She watched him take off his boots and socks, then stretch his toes toward the fire. Beautiful toes, long and straight, that had carried him thousands of steps to build her this sanctuary.

There had been a time when his mother would have kissed and tickled the baby roundness of them. If Emma gave up this wonderful home and moved to California, Matt would give her a chubby little baby to love and tickle.

At the beginning of summer, that would have been the last star she would have wished upon. Now, well, she didn't know anything anymore.

"Is Lucy feeling any better?" she asked.

"Still got a bellyache, but she fell asleep."

"It isn't like her to refuse to eat her dinner."

Matt rubbed his hands over his face, then shook out his hair. The fire's glow caught the bristle of a day's growth of beard and burnished it with golden lights.

"You didn't do much with yours, either. I suppose it's the same grief gnawing at the both of you. Pearl was a good old horse, there's none to say she wasn't," he said.

"She wasn't so old." She rocked in her chair and crossed her arms. "Matt, my troubles aren't the same as Lucy's. Does she even know that you are leaving in the morning?"

"No. I tried to tell her, but the words to make her understand wouldn't come." Matt rocked forward, planted his elbows on his knees and stared down at his feet. "Emma, would my leaving grieve you?"

"How can you ask? You know how fond I've grown of all of you."

Matt looked up, straight into her eyes. "That's not what I'm asking and you know it…. Will you grieve for me?"

The fool man! Did he want a declaration now, when tomorrow morning he would be riding off and taking her heart with him? Lordy, but she might be grieving more than this house could comfort.

"You'll be on the train long before I have a need to be grieving, Matthew Suede." He started to speak, but she hurried on saying anything that popped into her mind, anything to keep him from lingering here in such great danger. "I have a plan. I'll go into town and make a ruckus of some kind near wherever Hawker is. I'll call out for the doctor. Maybe I'll say you cut your hand on a bottle of Orange Lilly and you're half bled to death. I—"

"Hold on a minute, darlin'." He scooped up her hands and rubbed his rough thumbs across her knuckles. "You know that's not what I was asking."

"It's got to be the morning train." Emma tried to snatch her hands back before he noticed their trembling, but he held firm and brought them to his lips. He didn't kiss her fingers but held them to his mouth. He took a long slow breath. "I'll say that…that…wolves—or I'll faint dead away in Hawker's arms of some fright…that should keep him busy until—"

"Emma." His breath washed over her knuckles. "Why would your grief not be the same as Lucy's?"

"I've become fond of you." There was no sense in denying what he must see so plainly on her face. "There's no point in denying that I'll miss you."

"Fond, is it?" He slipped off his chair and onto his knees. Somehow he ended up kneeling between her spread thighs. Yards of fabric and petticoats weren't enough of a barrier to keep her from feeling the heat of him.

He dropped her hands and cupped her face in his palms.

"I suppose fond is what you feel for Red or Billy or a dozen folks in town." He skimmed his thumb along her lower lip. She closed her eyes against the draw of him. "Since you won't tell me true, I'll tell you how I feel."

Her eyes flew open.

"Don't, Matt, don't." She shook her head. "You'll be leaving in the morning."

"Tell me how you feel…about me."

She leaned forward, touching her forehead to his, squeezing her eyes shut and hiding the truth. "If I tell you, it might hold you here. You'd be killed."

He sighed; his breath warmed her lips. His scent shot straight to her heart. As long as she lived she'd never forget the way of him. Wild prairie and horses combined with leather and a bit of smoke from the fire all overpowered by the knee-weakening scent of male.

He found her hand, drew it to his mouth and kissed the wedding band. His gaze held her, demanding her soul.

"I love you," he whispered, warming the gold. "If that changes what happens tomorrow, so be it…. I love you, Emma."

Emma tasted the salt of a tear on her mouth and wondered which one of them it had come from.

"My grief is that I'll be losing something precious, and I can't choose what it will be." Emma wiped the moisture from her lip. Matt's eyes welled, but so did hers. "Come tomorrow, whatever happens, my heart will break."

She slipped out of the chair. Heart to heart with Matt, she buried her face in his shoulder.

"I do love you, Matt," she whispered into his shirt, and then she began to cry.

Matt rocked her for a moment, then held her at arm's length. He looked at her a long time, but didn't speak.

He unbuttoned his shirt, took her hand and placed it over his heart.

Fire-burnished hair rustled across his open collar when he reached for the buttons of her dress.

He popped them open one by one and spread her dress wide. Work-worn fingers plucked the tiny blue bow that fastened her shift. A couple of tugs at the lacy fabric left her breasts exposed.

The air in her lungs seemed too heavy to breathe.

Her heart beat too quickly not to show, but his heart beat the same way. She felt the runaway thrum of it under her fingertips.

With fingers that could as easily rope a steer as wipe away a tear, he touched her chest. He traced the bottom curve of her breast then brushed his thumb across her nipple, all the while gazing at her bare flesh as though that, too, was a caress.

At last he pressed his calloused palm over her heart, then lifted his gaze to her eyes.

"Bone of my bone," he whispered. "Flesh of my flesh."

He kissed her, a slow, deep kiss.

"Don't worry, darlin'." He buttoned her dress, stood up and drew her along with him. "Whatever tomorrow brings, we will face it together. When we've got things sorted out, we'll—" He nodded toward her bedroom.

This was all wrong. There was nothing to be sorted out except keeping Matt alive until he boarded the train.

And yet the moment they had just shared was nothing less than a joining of souls. Like wedding vows spoken all over again. And she had given herself over to them; the words Matt had recited were true.

She touched her lips with trembling fingers and tasted the promise of her future.

Matt had no more than opened the door to go to his bed in the soddie when a hacking sound came from Lucy's bedroom. "Papa, Mama! I throwed up!" Lucy's little voice wept. Whatever that future held, it would have to wait.

Chapter Twelve

"My tummy hurts, Papa."

"It'll feel better by morning, baby." Matt's stomach turned a flip or two, as well. "Close your eyes now. Try to sleep."

"She probably ate something that didn't agree with her." Emma stood beside the door with the soiled bedding wadded in her arms. "It isn't uncommon in children."

She gave him an encouraging smile, then continued down the hall. He listened to her footsteps brushing against the floor as she walked.

They had left important decisions hanging between them. Lucy's illness would hold things up for a bit.

One thing was sure, only death would part him from his wife now. That was the vow. Whatever paths he and Emma took, those words would guide him.

Matt smoothed the blanket across Lucy's slender shoulders. She looked so tiny in the big bed, so helpless and pale in the lamplight. He touched her cheek, fresh with a frosting of new freckles. Her skin felt dry but not hot. No fever was a good thing, he supposed.

Emma had come up so quietly in her stocking feet that he hadn't noticed her light steps crossing the room. She sat down on the bed beside Lucy with a glass of water in her hand. "Stomach complaints are common with children. Likely by morning she'll be better." The glass trembled slightly in her hand. She glanced at him. Her worried look said something else. "But there's the cholera…."

"It's only a stomach complaint. She's had them before."

He wouldn't let it be anything else. They all had been down with belly issues at one time or another and bounded right back. Morning would put the sparkle right back in Lucy's eyes.

"We'll need to make sure she drinks," Emma said, touching Lucy's hair to get her attention. "Sit up, sweetheart. You have to drink this."

"No! It hurts to drink." She burrowed under the blanket until only a blond curl gave away her presence.

Matt peeled the cover away and lifted Lucy onto his lap. Her toes peeked out from under her nightgown, as pale as her face.

"This might not stay down, so be ready," Emma instructed.

Lucy drank half the water, then squirmed off his lap and burrowed back into her woolen cave.

A bedspring squeaked when Emma got up. The fabric of her skirt rustled against her legs when she walked across the room.

Lucy's breathing seemed slow and even. Since sleep was what she needed most, Matt rose carefully from the bed and followed Emma out of the room.

He'd thought to find her in the kitchen washing the

glass, or maybe running her fingers over her stove with wonder, as she often did. He thought to see her peering out of the window, looking at her land by the glow of the moon with that satisfied smile tugging her lips into a pretty bow, or maybe watching for Pearl.

Instead, he found her collapsed into a chair at the table with her head buried in her arms. Her hair twisted down her back and over her shoulders.

He knelt beside her and brushed away enough hair to see the side of her face.

A gust of wind buffeted the window, rattling the glass.

Emma sat up straight and pressed her hands to her cheeks as though to brush away tears, but her eyes were dry.

"Emma, you look worn through." She tangled her fingers together on the table. He covered them with one of his hands and frowned at the tense cold knot beneath his palm. "Go on to bed. I'll watch over Lucy."

"Tell me about California. Is it really paradise on earth?"

He studied her face, looking for a spark of eagerness at the thought of moving there. Emma glanced at her stove and spread her fingers on the table where she served the tastiest food in the county. When she glanced at the "Home Sweet Home" frilly that she had crocheted and hung over the kitchen door, her eyes misted.

"So my mother says, but I've never been there. Seems to me this is paradise on earth."

She opened her mouth to answer, but Lucy's cry whispered down the hall.

Emma stood up and went ahead of him to her room.

* * *

Daylight had just brightened the plains with sunshine. Emma stood beside her laundry pot near the well, stirring Lucy's sheets, blankets and nightclothes in boiling water and lye. She dropped Matt's shirt into the pot with the rest.

Only a few hours from now, the train's whistle would be blowing. Matt and his family might have been on it, but all through the night Lucy had grown more ill. Her little body seemed to shrink in upon itself. Her skin appeared tissue thin and her robust complexion pasty.

Emma had never seen a child so taken with a stomach ailment. The strength leached out of her body with each heave of her belly. The poor little mite had quit whimpering about her misery just before sunrise, but clearly her silence didn't mean she was any better.

It was time to send for the doctor.

Red strode across the yard on legs grown longer and ganglier just overnight. He wore a hat, but the red spikes of his hair stuck out from under the brim like straw.

"I'll finish up the washing if you want to go inside and tend to Lucy."

"You're a thoughtful boy, Red." She had to reach up to pat his cheek. At the beginning of summer he'd been no more than half a head taller than she was. "It would do Matt good to get out of that room and get a breath of air."

With each step across the yard, she said a prayer that Lucy would be better, that the pink would be restored to her cheeks and the water in the glass beside her bed would be empty.

"Company's coming!" Red hollered.

Emma whirled on the top step of the porch. Company or a killer?

She shaded her eyes from the glare of the morning sun and squinted at the line of dust approaching the homestead. After a moment the painted wheels of the Sizeloffs' wagon rolled into view.

Her heart rolled in her chest. Just behind Rachael, cradling baby Maude in her arms, Charlie jumped and waved.

Praise and glory! At the back of the wagon, a horse was tethered.

"Pearl!" Emma shouted. She raced down the steps without feeling them.

Red dropped his stirring paddle and ran past her. He whooped and whistled, running and waving his arms. His hat blew off his head and bounced in the dirt. The screen door banged closed, but she didn't look back to see who had come out.

From a hundred yards off Pearl lifted her nose in the air and whinnied.

"I'm here, Pearl! I'm coming!" Emma's skirts tangled about her ankles. She grasped the hem and yanked it up to her knees. Decorum had no claim on her when her beloved Pearl had come back from the dead.

Charlie untied the lead securing Pearl to the wagon. "Go on girl, you're home," he called out.

Free of the fancy-wheeled wagon, Pearl trotted in a circle. She lifted her nose to scent the air, then pranced toward Emma.

"Oh, you wonderful horse." She touched Pearl's neck with splayed fingers. When she didn't find any burns or injuries she hugged tight with both arms. "You good, brave friend."

"Her mane's singed a bit," Billy announced, squeezing between Emma and Red and running his fingers through the dirty mass. "Her tail took the worst of it, but she seems whole enough."

"God be praised!" Emma heard Rachael declare, climbing down from the wagon. "We didn't know what to think when your horse showed up at the livery alone and singed."

"It was past dark when she wandered in," Joseph Sizeloff said, hurrying after his wife. A smile of relief shone out from under his mustache. "Jesse searched every shop and decent place in town."

"When Lenore Pendragon told him that her father had left you to perish out on the road we all thought the worst." Rachael gathered her tight in one arm. Little Maudie squeaked between them. "Praise be is all I can say."

"Poor Jesse is out there searching the burned areas right now," Joseph said. "Woody Vance, too."

"The town's abuzz over the matter, and that's a fact," Charlie stated, wiggling and hopping, apparently eager to be a part of Emma being found safe at home.

Princess and Fluffy bounded out of the corral. They ran in circles barking at one thing, then another. They spotted Charlie, charged and toppled him with their jumping.

He began to wrestle, rolling on the ground and laughing when suddenly he looked up with a frown. "Where's Lucy?"

"She's inside with Matt," Emma said. "She's not feeling well."

"Been heaving her stomach all night long." Red

yanked a pup off Charlie and pointed for it to scoot back to the barn.

"I've never tended a child so sick of a stomach complaint." Pearl chuffed at Emma's ribs. She stroked the horse's long jaw. "We're about to send for the doctor."

"Come on, Pearl." Billy took her tether. "Let's get you something to eat and give you a good look over while the women see to Lucy."

"Would you look at her, Rachael?" Emma asked. "I'm worried that this is no common ailment."

"Can I come, too, Ma?"

"Not this time, son." Rachael handed the baby to her husband. "You wait here with your pa until we know what ails Lucy."

A shiver of unease crept up Emma's spine. Rachael Sizeloff, an experienced mother who had prayed at the sickbeds of many people, didn't want Charlie to come near Lucy.

Oh, mercy! Emma led the way up the steps to the house and across the porch. She prayed that the preacher's caution was for safety's sake alone and that she didn't really believe there was anything to be alarmed about.

Since Lucy likely needed a prayer, Matt got up from the bed and let Preacher Sizeloff sit in the spot he had occupied for the past eight hours straight.

Emma stood in the doorway with her arms folded tight across her middle. The absence of a smile worried him as much as Rachael Sizeloff's frown when she bent low over Lucy and murmured into her pale ear.

Matt walked to the doorway where Emma stood, biting her lower lip. To comfort himself he gathered her up in his arms and rubbed his cheek on top of her head.

"I'm pleased that Pearl came home," he whispered. He felt her hair shift under his jaw when she nodded.

"Lucy's going to be just fine," she murmured low. "I'm sure Rachael is going to tell us just that."

The preacher cradled Lucy's cheek in the palm of her hand.

"Where does it hurt, little Miss Lucy?" She picked up the tiny hand that had seemed to go from plump and pink to thin and blue just overnight.

"My back and my legs." Matt had to strain to hear. Her voice had grown faint. "But mostly my tummy."

"What about here, on your arms, does this hurt, sweetie?"

Lucy nodded.

"I saw your pups outside. My, but they've grown half as big as their mother."

"Mama won't let them come in the house." Emma's shoulders sagged under his arms.

"You try and get some rest. I need to have a word with your mama and papa."

Before she stood, the preacher bent her lips close to Lucy's ear and whispered something. Matt couldn't hear much, but he thought he caught the words *pup* and *house*.

Rachael waved her hands at Emma and Matt, shooing them into the parlor as if they were a pair of wandering chickens. She shut Lucy's door behind her.

Red leaned against the front doorjamb with one foot on the porch and one in the parlor. He looked like a shadow against the glow of morning.

Matt stared at the preacher and knew that Emma and

Red did, as well. Even though she didn't have any medical training beyond motherhood, she had spent hours at the bedsides of the sick, comforting and praying. She would know when someone was deeply ill.

"I agree, you should send for Doc Brown...right away." She touched Matt's elbow and looked at him with worry creasing her eyes. "I can't be sure, but it could be the infantile cholera."

The floor shifted beneath his feet. Children died of the cholera! Some lived through it...but some didn't.

"Lucy's strong—she'll be fine," Emma said with confidence, but her fingers trembled on his arm.

"Day before yesterday she was fine. Right now she's not like I've ever seen her.... I'm going for the doctor," Matt said.

"You can't!" Emma leaped for the door. Crowding in beside Red, she set her legs wide and clamped her hands down on her waist. "You can't go to town!"

She wouldn't be much to pick up and set to the side, so he took a step forward.

Mrs. Sizeloff's hand, touching his sleeve, halted him. "She's right. Hawker's in town."

"Hawker doesn't count for much right now."

"Emma's right, Matt. If that no-good shoots you, how will you bring back the doctor?" Mrs. Sizeloff asked.

Matt was sick of the threat of Hawker hanging over his every move. Even moving to California was giving in to the man. But Preacher Sizeloff had a valid point. Setting things to right had no place right now. Only Lucy mattered.

When she was well, Hawker would have to be dealt with. No one that he loved was safe while the man breathed.

"I'll go!" Red spun about, but Matt caught the back of his vest.

"I'll tie you to the barn door if you try."

"Nobody needs to get killed to get the doctor here." The preacher shook her head. "My Josie has to take the children home, anyway. He can send out Doc Brown."

"The wagon will slow your husband down." Cousin Billy popped his head through the open parlor window. "I'll take Thunder and have the doc back in no time."

"I'd thank you for that, cousin."

Billy's offer gave Matt heart. He wasn't alone in this trial. Family was worth everything. A man could live in the middle of a field with no shelter at all more easily than trying to face what the world heaped on him without them. They were worth every sacrifice.

Emma went to the open window and peered out, watching Billy run full speed toward the corral.

Was she thinking the same thing? That hearts bound in loyalty were the best part of life.

"I'll go sit with Lucy and pray. We don't need to wait on Doc Brown for that," Rachael Sizeloff declared.

Matt expected Emma to follow the preacher into the sickroom, but instead, she pushed past Red and out onto the front porch.

"Princess!" she called. "Fluffy!"

The dogs came bounding toward the front door, stirring up a small twister's worth of dirt in the process. It collected on their fur like a second coat.

Emma stood aside when they gamboled past.

"Go on, go to Lucy," she murmured, but the pups were already on their way. Princess left four scratches on the floor scrambling for footing on the smooth wood. Fluffy bounded over the back of the couch, rolled on the cushions and deposited a mat of black fur before she tumbled off and drooled on the floor.

"Go on, you two, get in there and make Lucy feel better," Emma said.

She ought to be angry as a hornet now that the dogs had left their mark on her precious house. It more than frightened him that she allowed it.

Lord, how he loved the woman.

Emma stood beside the corral fence. Clouds rode low over the earth, painted orange and crimson by the setting sun. She watched the changing hues ride over the land—her land, every weed and piece of gravel. She breathed in a lungful of twilight air. It felt fresh and cleansing.

Fall was pushing summer into the past. Each night grew a little cooler than the one before. Time had run out so quickly and now her life balanced on a pinhead. Her beloved land, or the man she loved?

She couldn't think of that now. There was only Lucy, her baby, to be considered.

"Come over here, Pearl!" she called.

Thunder twitched his ears. He sauntered behind Pearl, nudging her flank with his nose when they reached the fence.

"I have both of you to thank for my life."

Pearl snorted. "All right, Matt, too." She stroked a brown face and then a black one. She reached into the pocket of her apron, pulled out a pair of apples and fed one to Pearl and one to Thunder.

Emma nuzzled her nose into Pearl's singed mane. No matter how she longed to have the summer back and spend it loving her husband, fall was at hand and Lucy needed tending.

"Doc Brown is spending the night. He's going to show me what to do for Lucy."

Boisterous wind caught her skirt and whipped it about. Chilly fingers pinched her arms when the gust pierced the sleeves of her dress. She shivered and rubbed her hands over her arms.

As if by magic, her shawl settled over her shoulders. Matt's big body stood close behind her and blocked the draft. He wrapped his arms about her and drew her against his chest.

"How many children survive this, do you think?" His voice rumbled next to her back, deep and worried. "Half?"

"Maybe, but Lucy's strong and that will go in her favor." A shiver traced through Matt's body. Emma felt it and patted his hands where they crossed over her ribs. "I've heard of children recovering."

But none of those children had overtaken her defenses so completely. None of them had laid claim to her heart. None of them had been allowed to call her Mama.

"She'll be fine." Her voice would sound more convincing if it weren't shaking. "You'll sing to her to keep her spirits up and I'll make her drink broth and keep her bedding clean. Mrs. Sizeloff will pray."

"She'll be on the mend in no time. We might have to sit on her to keep her from running off to play in the creek before she's ready," Matt said.

"Oh, yes. She'll be down there searching for Mr. Hopp—" All of a sudden the thought of Lucy never getting out of the sickbed swelled a lump in her throat that she couldn't speak over.

She turned in Matt's arms, pressed her face into his shirt and gripped his vest with tight fists. How many tears could eyes shed in only a few days?

Matt buried his face in her hair. He rocked her, his breath warm against her scalp.

The very seconds ticking by seemed to ache. Minutes, heavy with foreboding, stretched out forever.

Matt drew in a deep, steadying breath.

"Lucy's going to be fine." His voice, suddenly firm, was a lasso strung about her. She grasped it and pulled away from the black imaginings consuming her.

She glanced up. His eyes looked like troubled pools, flooded but contained.

"Of course she will. We won't let it be any other way."

Chapter Thirteen

The teapot whistling on the stove woke Emma from a brief doze at the kitchen table. She lifted her head and gazed out the window. Dawn would be more than an hour away, judging by the deep hue of the sky.

She arched her back to ease the crick that had settled in it from her awkward nap in the chair.

All through the long night it had seemed that she'd done nothing but make tea in hopes that Lucy would swallow a gulp or two. According to the doctor, not getting enough to drink was the main threat to her weakening body. Her survival depended upon keeping her hydrated.

The doctor had done what he could, applying cold compresses to Lucy's stomach to keep the vomiting down and whispering words of encouragement to his tiny patient.

He'd shown Emma how to wrap Lucy in warm wet sheets and then rub her with cold towels. But the main thing was to get her to drink and keep it down.

Peppermint had always relieved the little ones she'd tended, so that's what she had been brewing all night long. The house smelled like the candy counter at Rath and Wright's.

She stood up and walked to the stove. Her legs felt cramped from the short nap at the table. What wouldn't she give to fill her copper tub with hot water and melt into it? That's just what she would do at the first sign of Lucy's recovery.

The kitchen door opened. Cold predawn air rushed in with Cousin Billy.

"Morning, Billy. I haven't got the coffee brewed yet, but it will only take a few minutes."

"Don't trouble yourself. I just wanted to see how Lucy's doing before I check the fences."

"No change. Matt's in the bedroom with her. Dr. Brown is resting in my room. The poor man hasn't had a break since you brought him here."

"I'll check back in a few hours."

Billy tugged on the brim of his hat. He closed the door and stepped onto the porch. Emma set down the teapot and rushed outside after him.

"Billy, wait." She closed the back door but still spoke only half a note above a whisper. "Did you see Hawker in town? Did anybody say anything about...well, you know?"

"I took a peek at him." Billy squeezed her elbow with his leather glove. "No need to worry, Emma. He's nothing more than any other mortal man."

"I saw him catch his hat right out of the air. He's fast with his hands. What if he comes out here? Matt's so tired and worn through he wouldn't stand a chance."

"Matt would have caught his hat before it ever let fly off his head. If you're worried about Hawker coming here, don't be. My cousin protects what is his own."

"That's what I'm afraid of."

A rooster crowed in the barn. In another hour the sun would pop over the horizon. Billy let go of her elbow and started down the steps as though the bird had been his signal to get to work.

"Emma." Billy turned at the bottom step, looking up. "I apologize for Woody."

"For Woody? Why on earth would you?"

"It was me that set you up to pair with him." Billy picked at a splinter in the handrail of the steps. "Any fool can see that it was you and Matt all along."

"Maybe you were right about me needing a man." Emma came down the steps, stopping on the last one so that she was eye to eye with Billy. She kissed his cheek. "You only misjudged the one I needed."

"I'm glad of that, cousin." He grinned, then strode toward the barn.

Matt was a lucky man to have a cousin as devoted as Billy. They had grown up as close as brothers. She'd never spent much thought or regret on her past, but watching Matt's family over the summer made her wonder. What might it have been like to grow up with someone of her own?

Mercy, but this was no time for fanciful yearnings. She had tea to force down a resisting child's throat. She'd think about those things later, when Lucy was well and she had an hour to soak in her big brass tub.

It felt like a betrayal to leave Lucy's sickroom. The only reason Matt did it was that Emma had forced a cup of coffee into his hand and told him he was making Doc Brown nervous.

"He can take better care of Lucy without you hanging

over the bed." She'd gently herded him and his steaming cup from the room. "Go outside and breathe some fresh air before the doctor has another patient to tend to."

In the parlor Matt was surprised to see the preacher sitting on the couch with her hands folded in her lap, her head bent low in either sleep or prayer. She looked up when his boots scraped the floor.

"Good morning, Mrs. Sizeloff," his mouth said out of habit, but this was far from a good morning. Even though the sun shone brightly on the prairie grass and streamed in through the windows it might as well have been midnight. "You haven't been here all night, have you?"

Since he hadn't been out of Lucy's room in…how many hours, he'd lost track. It had been light when he'd last seen her and it was light again, with a night passing in between.

"Lands, no. Wouldn't Josie have a time trying to care for little Maudie by himself? Infants aren't the most agreeable folks if they're hungry."

He remembered that. Lucy used to raise a fuss if her bottle wasn't at her lips the moment she needed to eat. Mrs. Sizeloff would be even more tied to her infant, since the baby was likely a nursling.

"It was good of you to come back. Looks like we need all the prayers the good Lord will listen to."

"He's got a wonderfully big ear. So do I." She got up from the couch in a rustle of brown plaid. "Let's take a walk in the sunshine and you can tell me what the doc thinks."

Morning light was blinding after having spent so much time in a darkened sickroom. Without his hat to shade his eyes, he had to stare at the ground.

That suited him fine, since the happy blue of the sky looked too much like Lucy's eyes had only days ago, alive with laughter and health. It felt as if a stone weighted his heart when he looked into her eyes now.

He led the preacher toward the well where the shade under the roof would give his vision some relief.

"Doc says there's not much change since last night, but I think Lucy's getting weaker. He's trying to keep her from going into decline. If that happens—" Some words just shouldn't be said—they hurt worse than physical pain. "There won't be much hope."

"There's always hope."

Matt looked at the preacher's face. A blaze of white hair cut through the darker strands, streaking from her forehead to the bun tucked in a proper roll at her neck.

Folks in town said the streak had come from God. She'd asked him for it as a sign that a sick friend would recover from a terrible illness. According to the story, she'd got the streak and the friend had gotten well. He'd like to think the tale was true. Maybe she knew more about hope than he did.

"Sometimes things that seem bad turn around to be something wonderful," she said.

He didn't know what to say about that. He'd seen things that started bad get even worse.

"Take your own life, for example." The doubt must have shown on his face. She smiled and patted his arm where it crossed his chest. "It's not often a man goes from robbing a bank to falling in love and legally wed in the space of an hour."

He sputtered, or gasped. He must have gone red as sunset, maybe pale as the moon. He sure couldn't think of a blessed thing to say. A man couldn't very well lie to the person who had spent untold hours praying for his daughter.

"It wasn't so hard to figure out." A chuckle shook her shoulders. She planted her hands at her waist and shuffled the dirt with the toe of her shoe. "I believe in hope, Matt. I also believe that love can happen in a minute."

The woman might be a dove in God's service, but she had the eyes and instincts of a hawk. He still couldn't figure out what to say, so he offered her water.

"No, thank you," she said, her eyes lighting with laughter. "There's no call to look so green about the ears. Since I haven't let on to the law about it by now, I suppose you are safe from me...and Josie, too. There are a few things I don't understand, though, like why you only took ten percent. It's a subject that's kept my husband and me in conversation for many a night beside the fire. And then there's Emma, of course. I would guess there's an interesting story to be told there, if you had a mind to tell it."

"Since you got the half of it, you might as well know the whole thing, so you don't go believing I'm a common thief."

He sat on the well and invited the preacher to do the same. Even though she had claimed not to need a drink, he could use a long one to tell what was more of a confession than a story.

He told her about the ten percent for Lucy. That easing of his conscience hadn't stunned her one bit. She'd only nodded and stated that the sin had been on Lawrence Pendragon's soul, not Matt's.

That had always been his belief, but it was a comfort to have it confirmed by someone who was a professional in the wrongs and rights of spiritual matters.

As far as love in an hour? He shrugged his shoulders. "Emma didn't love me when you married us. We'd only just met."

"Mercy, Matt. I suppose everyone in the land office figured that."

"The sheriff must have believed us. Otherwise, he'd have strung me up."

"I imagine that's what he thought he did. But then with you and your bride looking so lovesick at each other, and that kiss…! Well, no one could say otherwise."

"My wife is quite a woman."

"Whether you loved each other then or not, I'd say you love each other now."

How much did a man reveal to his wife's friend, preacher or not?

"We do." Matt stood up. He liked speaking with Mrs. Sizeloff. It was a comfort to be able to say some things out loud. But maybe he'd been away from Lucy for too long. "But there are some issues with Hawker that need to be set straight."

"By violence?" she asked, a deep frown creasing her brow.

"Shoot, Mrs. Sizeloff, maybe. Right now, with things the way they are, my family is in danger." He felt the threat to his bones. Even though he wasn't wearing his gun his hand touched the spot where it would be.

"You could pack up your family and go away."

"I thought so at one time. I had hoped to convince Emma to come to California with me, but this land and her house mean the world to her. I can't ask her to leave it behind."

"Emma would love California, as well. I hear it's paradise on earth."

"I've heard the same, but as far as my wife is concerned, this hundred and sixty acres is paradise on earth. I can't say I disagree." Matt glanced toward the house, nervous that something might change while he was chatting.

"As wonderful as home can be, paradise isn't a spot on a map. No sir, what I believe is that it is a place in the heart."

"Family ties?" He believed the same.

The preacher stood up. She smoothed her palm over the streak in her hair, then fluffed out her skirt.

"Yes, exactly so," she said with a pivot toward the house. "Don't you give up hope. You'll find a way out of this mess."

A sulking mass of clouds gathered on the western horizon and obscured the first sunset of autumn.

The long day finally ended with Lucy getting no better. The good doctor, with great reluctance, had gone back to Dodge to set a cowboy's broken arm.

Emma stood on the porch and gazed across the darkening prairie, watching for his return. Cold wind snapped the hem of her skirt. She drew her shawl tight against the chill. Dr. Brown had expected to return near nightfall and she had made sure to keep a plate of supper warming on the stove for him.

Inside, the house was too quiet. Outside, the land stretched away dim and ominous. When the doctor had departed, Rachael had tied her horse to the back of his buggy and ridden back to Dodge beside him. She, too, had been hesitant to return to town, but the demands of an infant had first claim on her time.

"I'll be back in the morning...sooner if I'm needed," she had vowed.

Emma shivered when a nippy gust pressed her backward a step on the porch, but she wasn't sure that the trembling was due to the draft.

Needing the preacher sooner than dawn didn't bear thinking of. To hear those words spoken had been nearly more than she could stand. The only reason she hadn't collapsed in a weeping heap when she had heard them was that Matt had been standing beside her.

He'd barely breathed. His shoulders had straightened, then stiffened. Standing so close, she'd felt a shiver run over his body. Even though his jaw had clenched and flexed, he hadn't cried out at the grievous thought.

That thought haunted everyone's mind, for sure, but until noon today, no one had spoken the words aloud.

What nearly made her knees buckle seemed to leave Matt unshaken. She knew he must be terrified, but he had stood taller and acted braver than any man she'd ever met.

The long hours between noon and now had been bearable only because of Matt's strength. She'd show him the same grit of spirit even though she felt fragile.

Since the doc wouldn't appear on the road for all her staring at it, she went back inside the house. The teapot whistled for her attention, so she brewed up one more cup of peppermint tea that Lucy would not drink.

Earlier in the day the poor child would drink what was put in front of her lips then promptly lose it into a pan. Over the aching hours of the afternoon she had stopped doing even that. She'd turned her pale face toward the pillow and refused even the tiniest of sips.

Since liquid was what Lucy needed to stay alive, Emma carried the steaming mug into the bedroom with a smile of confidence. Unfortunately, the smile would soothe only Matt, since Lucy rarely opened her eyes anymore.

He sat in a rocking chair beside the window holding Lucy. His arms looked part strength, part tenderness drawing her close to his heart. The color of his shirt had deepened to a dark blue plaid where it had become soaked from the warm wet sheet tucked about her.

The chair rocked against the floor with a creak. Matt sang the song about Utah Carl saving the life of little Lenore. Emma remembered the song from that not so long ago night that Matt had driven her out to her homestead. Emma understood now that the song had been about Lucy's father.

Did Matt sing it to Lucy because he believed that father and daughter would be together soon? Emma choked back a groan. She wasn't ready to say goodbye to Lucy in such a way.

Waving goodbye from the station platform would have been sorrow enough. To lose Lucy to the grave would be unbearable.

Matt hummed for a moment, then looked up.

"I can't tell if she hears me or not."

Emma sat on the bed, shoving aside Princess to make room. The dog stood up, followed its tail in a circle, then settled beside Fluffy.

"I hear you, Papa."

Lucy's voice sounded thin and dry. Matt dipped his ear close to her tiny cracked lips. When she said no more he thumped his head against the back of the rocker with a long slow sigh.

Emma slipped to the floor in front of the rocker.

"Its Mama, baby. You've got to try and drink some of this tea." She stroked the damp curls off Lucy's forehead and wished that the moisture had not come from the sheet, but from sweet healthy sweat. "Please, take just a sip."

Lucy shook her head once, weakly.

Emma took a small square of clean cotton from the pocket of her apron. She dipped it in the tea.

"Open her mouth and see if she'll suck on this. Maybe enough will trickle down her throat to do her some good." She sat back on her heels and watched Matt press the dripping cloth to Lucy's lips. He dabbed her mouth to moisten it then slipped the peppermint rag into her mouth

"She's taking it." The first smile she'd seen in more hours than she wanted to count tipped the corners of Matt's lips.

"Let's try it again," she said.

She dipped the rag into the tea three more times and Lucy sucked like a baby with her bottle.

"We'd better make that enough for now."

"Pray God it stays down," Matt said.

She touched his knee and nodded. "It will. This time it will."

There was no way of knowing that, but sounding sure made her spine a little stiffer and her voice a bit firmer.

"Rachael wonders if it's water that makes the children come down with this infantile cholera." She stood up, moved Princess's tail out of the way and sat once more upon the bed.

Thunder clapped in the distance. The sudden bang rattled the shutters at the window.

"The water looks clean enough. I wonder what would cause it to make folks sick." Matt resettled Lucy in his arms, then drew her limp little body closer in the sodden sheet. A shiver caught his shoulders. He would be cold with his own clothing getting wet. Maybe in his concern for Lucy he didn't notice it, or maybe he didn't feel it worth the mention.

"I can't figure it, but Rachael says the Chinese don't get cholera and they don't drink water, only tea," she said.

Rain pelted the window, driven by sidelong wind.

Princess laid her warm black head on Emma's lap and whined. The dogs had grown as listless as their young mistress. Emma traced a line with her finger from the tip of the pup's nose to the gentle slope of her head. "Good pup."

"Rachael has lived all over the place." Lightning blanched the inside of the room in stark light for an instant before thunder crashed over the house. Emma felt the dog tense and whine until the room once again glowed with the soft light of the oil lamp. "She says whenever her husband gets the call to move on, they pack up the family and go."

"They've been in Dodge for some years now." Matt slowed his rocking to a creakless tilt. "I expect there's plenty of souls need saving right here without having to move on."

"That must be a relief to her." Emma listened to heavy rain pulse and ripple across the roof. "Getting to put down roots someplace."

"I reckon she'd tell you her roots aren't in any kind of soil, but in her family's heart."

There was a good chance that was the very thing Rachael would say.

What good did those kinds of roots do Emma, now? As soon as Lucy was well, and she would be, heartache in one form or another would shatter her.

Buggy wheels crunched outside, passing the window.

Emma shooed the dogs away from the bed. "That must be Doc Brown."

Matt laid Lucy down in the center of the mattress and trailed his finger over her sunken cheek before he straightened.

"I'll go see to his horse."

"He'll want to dry off and have a bite to eat." Emma took a step toward the door, but Matt caught her arm.

"Whatever happens…" Emma's shoulder grazed his chest. She felt his damp shirt brush against her arm with his breathing. "I'm not sorry you caught me in the livery that day."

"I'm not sorry, either."

He kissed her.

One and a half heartbeats later he dashed out to meet the doctor.

Piano music, jangling out of the open door of the Long Branch, wasn't a whit muffled by the rain pounding Front Street to mud.

Red pressed his back against the wall of the store on the opposite side of the street. Anyone gazing out of the saloon would not notice him standing under the porch overhang with rain sluicing off the roof and pelting the toes of his boots.

Blamed if the rectangle of light coming out of the saloon's door did anything but let fresh air in and smoke rings out. For observing what went on inside, it wasn't much. How was he to get a glimpse of Hawker if he didn't get any closer than this?

Matt had forbidden him to go inside any of the saloons in town. He'd forbidden him to come to town at all. Next thing, Matt would forbid him to even think a wicked thought.

There would be hell to pay if he got caught standing here, so why not move a little closer, as long as he might have to pay for the crime, anyway?

Since he was near the size of a grown man, he could stand outside the door with his hat pulled low, as if he was a gambler taking a break from his winning streak. That way, he'd be able to see most of what went on inside.

Odds were against anyone in there recognizing him. Since respectable folk were cozied up in their homes at this hour, he wasn't likely to get caught.

With the chances of being found out slim, Red took long bold steps through the muck and up the steps to the Long Branch.

Sure was a party going on inside there. It would be a fine thing to be able to join in if he was of a mood, but celebrating wasn't much in his heart. With Lucy sick near to death and Matt and Emma near lovesick to death, a frolicking time didn't seem fitting.

With a deep tug on the brim of his hat he took up his bored-gambler stance beside the door. A steady drip of water from his Stetson ticked against his vest. He took off his gloves and shoved them into his rear pocket. That made his fingers cold, but a gambler wouldn't likely be standing about wearing homestead gloves.

He'd heard enough descriptions of Hawker to know that the killer was of medium height and bald as a door-knob. He might be the man sitting face toward the door no more than twenty feet in.

The fellow was thick around the middle, just as Emma had described him, and shifted the cards in his hands as quickly as Red's eyes could follow.

He'd be a match for Matt if it ever came to it.

Red blew on his chilly fingers. A man of cards would do that so as not to let his luck run cold. Someday, if he lived through the thing he had to do, he'd try his luck at a game or two.

He didn't hear the footsteps coming up the steps, but he heard the voice whispering in his ear clearly enough.

"You young saphead, what are you doing hanging outside the saloon in the rain?"

"You're out here, too, Jesse, so I guess I'm no more of a saphead than you are."

"I've got a legitimate reason to be out." Jesse tugged on his elbow, pulling him out of eyesight of the saloon door. "You're here looking for trouble."

"That's not exactly so. I'm looking to end trouble, is all." How would he do that now, with Jesse showing up to make sure he didn't?

"Any fool can see that you're peeking in at Hawker. No wonder Matt worries about you so."

"No one needs to worry about me. I'm near grown and fast as any man."

"You're too dumb to know just how dumb you sound." Jesse took three steps down the boardwalk, then turned back. "You going to come to the livery and spend the night with me or just stand there and let the rain turn you into a drowned pup?"

"Ain't no pup." But the wetter he got, the colder he got. The stove in the livery sounded inviting. Besides, if he called out Hawker tonight, as he wanted to, his trigger finger would be too stiff to do the job.

He fell in step beside Jesse, eager for the warmth of the stove and maybe even some dry clothes.

"How's Lucy faring?"

"Not good. Doc Brown is doing what he can, but I can't hardly stand to see her looking so weak and pitiful."

That was half the reason he had sneaked off. To see Lucy looking like a ghost broke his heart. Nothing was the same without her making things lively.

"Matt must be in a state," Jesse said.

"He tries to act like he isn't, but he was in a state before Lucy ever got sick."

"All this business with Hawker's got to be a strain."

Jesse glanced over his shoulder at the saloon a block back.

"That's part of it, for sure. The rest is that he wants Emma to go with us to California, but she won't leave her house…. Jesse, you got anything to eat in the livery—for folks, I mean?"

"I can keep you fed and warm, just so long as you agree to stay put. I won't have you hunting down Hawker during the night."

A block away, a yellow light shone from Jesse's room inside the livery. A full belly and a warm pile of straw to bed down on seemed more fitting at the moment than icy rain and justice.

"I'll stay put for now, but Jess, I'm the one who ought

to be facing Hawker." He could do it, too. With just a little practice he would be a faster draw than even Matt, and that was saying something. "Matt's only in this scrape because of me. If it hadn't been for me, he wouldn't have to go to California. He could stay here with Emma and be happy."

Rain pelted his face so hard that it stung. He bent his head and lengthened his strides toward the livery.

"You were even more of a child then than you are now. Matt made his choice, Red. He never regretted it and doesn't now."

That didn't change a thing. This was his fight. Once he took care of Hawker, Matt would be able to live the life he wanted with the woman he loved. He owed his stand-in father at least that much, likely a great deal more.

Besides, being young didn't mean being slow. Lots of boys made a name with their gun. Billy the Kid, for one.

Red ignored Matt's voice in his mind reminding him that The Kid was dead.

He would not end up dead. He would be the one to make everything come out right.

Chapter Fourteen

*D*ecline.

Seven ordinary letters—one word that he would rather die than hear.

Matt didn't die, though, even with the doctor standing beside Lucy's bed making the pronouncement.

Morning sun broke through the storm and scattered it toward the east, but there was no cheer in it. He felt numb. Fear surrounded his heart and squeezed. Only by locking his knees did he remain standing so that he could ask what was the worst that could happen now.

Emma slipped in under his arm. Her fingers trembled against his vest, so he hugged her close. Her dress felt as wet as his shirt from the many hours of wrapping Lucy in warm damp sheets.

"It doesn't always mean there's no hope." Doc Brown lifted his glasses away from his face and wiped his hand across his face. Two days' worth of beard stubble scraped beneath his palm with a hiss. "From here on out her little body has less to fight back with. The disease has the upper hand and it's harder for her to... but I've seen some make it that were even further into decline than Lucy is. Children are tough, for all they seem so small."

"Lucy is." Emma's voice barely whispered out of her lips, yet it sounded certain. She turned in the crook of his elbow and reached out, touching his cheek with her fingertips. "Mercy, that child surprises us day in and day out."

Lucy's mother had been strong, and so had her father, but they had long since been in the grave.

Emma's confidence rallied his sagging spirits only enough that they floated ankle-high in the gloomy room, which was a sight higher than they had been a second ago.

He cupped her face in his hands and kissed her forehead before he bent next to the bed.

"Lucy, darlin'. Did you hear the doc?" She lay so pale and silent on the bed that if it hadn't been for the shallow rise and fall of her thin ribs he would have thought the worst. "You don't have to go. You're a strong little girl, just like Mama says. Everyone's out in the parlor praying that you'll soon be stomping around in the creek looking for frogs."

Princess whined and laid her head over Lucy's arm. Fluffy gave a quiet yip and a half wag of her tail.

"Did you hear that, baby? I believe Fluffy and Princess just said a prayer in their own puppy way."

It may have been his imagination, but he thought he saw her head nod a fraction of an inch.

The fighter inside her hadn't given up, but her little body seemed to be fading by the moment. Unless something changed, unless something…

It was clear that there was nothing more he could do

for her. Maybe only ease her way out of this world with a song. He thought she might hear it, so he began a low croon even though it ripped from his heart and tasted bitter on his tongue.

The tone sounded shaky, as if his voice had grown too fearful to hold a common note. It stretched as thin as a tight string.

From behind he heard Emma choke on a single sob. All of a sudden he couldn't breathe. The walls darkened and closed in like a smothering, living thing.

"I've got to go out for a minute, darlin', but I'll be back. Don't you go anywhere, do you hear, baby? Don't go."

Matt dashed out of the sickroom and crossed the parlor without greeting Rachael or Joseph Sizeloff, who sat on the couch speaking in quiet tones with Jesse.

It was a surprise to see Jesse here at this time of morning, since no one had yet sent word of Lucy's decline.

Out on the porch Billy sat on the stoop whittling a six-inch piece of wood. Red, leaning against the house, gave him a quick glance then stared at his boots.

Greeting them would be polite, but the only thing he wanted was to get to the barn. There, in the privacy of shadows and the silence of shifting straw, he would give way to the fear that turned his courage to dust. If he didn't he might just burst open from the grief of it.

He'd let it go, then find the fortitude to go back inside. If his child needed him to hold her back from the grave with all his strength, that's what he'd do. If she needed him to let her go, to help ease her to the other side, he'd do that, too.

* * *

"Mrs. Suede…Emma, wake up."

The doctor's voice sounded far away, but the urgent pressure of his fingers on her shoulder roused her. Had she truly fallen asleep sitting on the floor beside the bed? If the tingling in her legs was any indication she'd been at it for some time.

"I must have dozed off for a moment," she mumbled, but didn't want to open her eyes, it seemed as if years had passed since she'd last had a solid night's sleep.

She cracked her eyelids open and glanced around the room. Matt hadn't returned yet, so not much time would have passed.

"There's someone asking for you."

Emma wiggled her toes to chase away the fuzzy feeling in them. If neighbors were calling to offer comfort they'd want something to eat, or maybe some tea, if she could stand to brew another cup.

She glanced up at the doctor's face to see him smiling.

"Mama." Lucy's voice sounded weak, but she spoke!

Emma spun about on her knee.

"Lucy!" She touched the small ashen cheek and smoothed back a tangle of curls from Lucy's forehead.

A quick glance up at the doctor told her what she wanted to know. His smile, stretching from one side of his face clear to the other, had to mean that Lucy would recover.

"You're going to be just fine, baby. Are you thirsty?" Lucy nodded, then glanced beside her on the mattress. "Mama, Fluffy and Princess are in the house…right on my bed."

Emma had to bend her ear low to hear. Lucy's voice

was no more than a whisper, but, praise be, she had despaired of ever hearing it again!

"They've been so worried. I suppose they can stay for a while." She wanted to cry and laugh all at once. Judging by the taste of wet salt on her tongue, she was doing both.

Lucy reached for her pups and was rewarded by a pair of wagging tails. Luckily the dogs recognized that their companion was still weak and didn't yip and trounce upon her.

"I'll go get you some tea."

"I'll take care of that, Mrs. Suede." The doctor looped his thumbs into the suspenders sagging from his shoulders and rocked back on his heels. His grin puffed his cheeks into pink circles of happiness. "You go on along and spread the good word to your husband."

This would be the best news she had ever passed on, but first there was something she wanted to say. Something that she had never said to a child. She bent close to Lucy's cheek and kissed it.

"I love you, baby. I love you so much."

"I love you too, Mama."

"I'll be right back." She tucked the blanket about Lucy and noticed with a swell of joy that the doctor had replaced the wet sheet with a nice dry one. "I'm going to go get Papa."

Lucy's chest rose and fell beneath her palm. Her gaze looked sleepy but not far away or unfocused, as it had been. She smiled, sighed, then fell promptly asleep.

Mercy, but should she be sleeping already?

"Lucy?" Emma cast a worried glance at Doc Brown, who had returned from the kitchen with the tea.

"Don't worry," he said. "It's a good healthy sleep. She'll be back to her old self sooner than you think."

Emma stood up, but had to let her bones settle. Even though she hadn't been beside the bed for that long the joints felt unnatural and the muscles stiff.

"I've got to tell Matt." She stomped her feet on the floor. Normal feeling flooded back into her toes. The rest of her limbs would take care of themselves in time. She couldn't wait for the tingling to subside. She had to give Matt the news before he broke with the worry.

"You go along. I'll be right here in case she wakes up." The doctor waved her toward the door. "Although I don't expect it for some time."

"Thank you." She flung her arms about his neck. Some words just didn't say enough.

Emma dashed through the parlor. At the front door she noticed the Sizeloffs, Jesse and Billy sitting on the couch, staring after her. She spun toward them but paused for only a heartbeat.

Down the front steps and across the yard, she ran as if her skirt had wings. Air, fresh with a snap of fall, whizzed past her cheeks. She barely felt the pebbles under her shoes.

She ran past the well, scattering squawking chickens.

She pushed open the barn door and leaned against it to catch her breath and give her eyes a moment to adjust to the dimness inside.

Where was Matt? The barn, with its empty stalls, seemed to be holding its breath. Even the dust motes in a beam of sunlight appeared to stand still. A single dove cooed in the rafters, breaking the silence and softening the gloom.

On the far wall, beside Pearl's stall door, a shadow shifted. Emma hurried forward.

Matt sagged against the gate with his arms resting on the top rail, his shoulders slumped and his head dipped low.

He must have heard her, but he didn't look up. She touched the back of his vest and felt a shiver race beneath her fingertips.

"Matt," she whispered.

He took a deep breath, straightened and turned to face her. Lord, but she couldn't remember ever seeing such misery in a face. Deep lines cut the corners of his mouth and his skin looked pale. His hair dragged about his face as though he were hiding behind it.

But his eyes looked the worst, appearing to have traveled the road to hell and back, and back wasn't any better than hell.

She reached up to brush away a strand of hair that had stuck to the corner of his mouth.

"You're trembling all over, Emma." His voice sounded so bleak that it must have passed beyond despair sometime back. He wiped one thumb across the moisture on her face. "Lucy's gone? My baby, she's—"

She shook her head. "Tears of joy. The doc says she's going to recover!"

For the longest time he stared down at her, as if he was stunned or didn't dare believe it.

"It's true, Matt."

All at once the moisture that had been lurking in his eyes for days let loose. It slipped down his cheeks, catching on the stubble of his beard and pooling at the corners of his lips.

His shoulders hitched inward. His arms, tight with

tension, drew her close and pressed her tight to his chest. He bent his head to her shoulder and wept quietly against her neck.

After a moment, his chest stilled. He raised his head, tipped it back and his lungs expanded.

"Yee-ha-a-a!" His shout disturbed the dove in the rafters and set it flapping about the barn. It darted out through the window in the hayloft with a twitter of alarm.

All of a sudden Emma's feet left the ground. Matt twirled her about, his arms braced about her back. Around and around he spun her, clearly as delirious with joy as she was.

She screeched, Matt whooped. When he stopped he didn't put her down. Eye to eye, winded breath mingling with winded breath, he grinned at her. He kissed her. Jubilation joined them. Love bound them.

Life without Matt would be dreary, no matter if she lived in a palace. With him, she could live in a hovel and be happy.

So there it was. Once made, her decision hurt but choosing the other way would have left her dead inside.

"I'm coming with you to California."

"Emma?" He set her down on the floor.

"Just as soon as Lucy is able to travel, we can go."

"Darlin', that's a hard choice. You ought to give it some time."

"Time won't make a difference…and it could kill you." She shook her head, more sure by the second that her decision was the only one she could make. "Everything has changed. I've made up my mind."

She hadn't expected him to frown. "Whatever happens, do you promise to stand by me, darlin'?"

"On the honor of our wedding vows." And at the cost of her home, but she meant it. "Let's get going—there's a little girl who's going to want to see her papa."

His grin returned, wide and bright enough to light the barn. Once again he kissed her. This time she tasted forever.

"Yee-haa!" He caught her hand and they ran toward the house together.

The deep silence of midnight settled down about the house. Health and hope brought the promise of new life to every quiet corner.

Hawker still waited in town. That was a problem he would deal with, but somehow, given everything that had happened, it didn't cast as large a shadow. Death had knocked on the homestead door and been sent packing. Would he be likely to show his wicked face again so soon?

Possibly life and death had no rules, but he wouldn't think about that just yet. For now, he was content to stand in the doorway of Lucy's bedroom and watch her gain strength in a healthy, deep sleep. Fluffy and Princess, flanking her on left and right, watched the easy rise and fall of her breathing.

An hour ago Emma had declared that she would spend the whole night in her big brass tub. She had begun to heat the water, but Matt had shooed her out of the kitchen and insisted on doing that chore himself. He owed her far more than a hot bath, but it would do for now.

Emma had worn herself through with nursing Lucy. It was a wonder that someone living in such a petite frame would have the energy to go on and on.

Of course, he'd known all along that Emma was a wonder. Even though she might deserve to spend the whole night long in the tub, the water would soon grow cold.

He hadn't heard a splash or a sigh in over half an hour. It wouldn't do for her to fall asleep and catch a chill. She might not like to have him peeking into her private bath, but who better than a husband to see to it?

Especially now that she had spoken her heart and he had spoken his. She was right about everything changing. He expected that he would hear an earful when she found out what those changes were going to be. He could only hope that she would keep her promise to stand beside him.

His Emma was not the type to go back on a vow, although she might consider it once she discovered that he had also made a decision.

Matt walked through the kitchen toward the door leading to the bathroom. Emma's blue-checkered apron hung on a peg beside the stove. A vase of late-blooming flowers sat square on the table.

He paused in the middle of the room and glanced about, noting the care with which she had placed all her treasured things. The scent of peppermint tea lingered in the lace curtains at the window.

He couldn't leave this place. The moon would fall smack out of the sky before he'd expect Emma to do it.

Matt opened the bathroom door and stepped inside. Just as he'd expected, Emma had fallen dead asleep in the water.

Her hair hung over the back of the tub, shimmering in the soft glow of the turned-down lamp. One arm was draped over the copper edge with a wet cloth mounded on the ground beneath her fingertips.

He felt a song rising in his throat. It seemed a lifetime ago that he had felt like singing, but the seduction of her body, reclining so bare and pink in the cool water, purely inspired him. He kept quiet, though, reluctant to wake her.

Lamplight flickered over her moist limbs, glinting where her flesh pebbled with a chill.

He knelt beside the tub.

"Emma," he whispered. She sighed. Her breasts seemed to swell and shimmer in the dim, lustrous light. "Darlin', wake up. The water's grown cold."

Words didn't seem to rouse her, so he touched her face where a loop of hair twisted over her cheek.

"Darlin'?"

He leaned forward and kissed her mouth, lingering longer at it than would be required to wake a sleeping beauty. Once more, her sigh lifted her bosom. Her cool, firm nipple grazed his arm where he had rolled his shirtsleeve up.

For all that she looked like a simmering feast, a treat he was willing to risk his life to get a taste of, she was beginning to shiver, even in the depths of an exhausted sleep.

"Come on, then, darlin'."

He plunged his arms into the water without remembering to shove both sleeves up past his elbows. He lifted his wife and gathered her close, then walked through the kitchen. At the hall, he turned toward Emma's bedroom.

Bathwater trickled from her flesh and dampened his pants and shirt.

Missing all the fussy clothing that women stuffed themselves into, she felt as light as a bag of dreams. It took no effort to peel back the flowery quilt and hold her snug to his chest at the same time.

He didn't want to put her down. Her thighs felt smooth under his coarse fingertips, like rose petals. She smelled like a rose, too, with nothing between her flesh and his nose but a little bit of air.

Laying a wet woman between the covers of her bed didn't seem wise, so he went to the bathroom and brought back two towels. He put one on the bed, then laid Emma gently down.

He dried her hands and rubbed the water off her arms. He wrapped her feet in the towel, first one then the other. He stroked the moisture from each pretty calf. Just north of her knee on her left leg he paused. Her sturdy, shapely limbs made him feel weak all over.

Or was it strong? It was hard to tell with his insides crashing around.

"You're the most beautiful woman I've ever seen, Emma Suede." He pressed the towel to her neck, then stroked downward over her breasts. The fabric was thick and scratchy, but the shape and the heat of her came up through it. "And I don't just mean on the outside."

He whisked the towel down her ribs and across her hips. It'd be best to get the quilt between her skin and his hands before he did something reproachable, like wake her up with his need to make her his, body as well as soul.

Emma was exhausted with all she had done to save his baby girl. She needed the healing sleep as much as Lucy did.

He'd have his wife, and soon, but it wouldn't be right unless she was awake.

He lifted the quilt from the foot of the bed. It settled about her with a whisper. It hugged her form with a caress.

"I love you, Emma. You can't imagine how much."

He stroked her cheek, then traced the curve of her head with his palm before he turned toward the door.

He hadn't taken a step from the bed when her cool fingers grabbed his hand.

"I love you, too," she whispered. "Don't go."

"You look like a woman in need of seducing, Mrs. Suede."

She grinned at him and tugged him down onto the bed. She flipped back the quilt and patted the mattress.

"Better get out of those damp clothes."

That was advice he didn't need. He tossed his vest and shirt onto the floor. The rest of what he had on went somewhere, but damned if he knew where.

In less time than it took to catch his breath, he slid in under the quilt. The corkscrew hair on his legs skimmed Emma's thighs. Satin sheets on a fancy bed wouldn't have felt as smooth as her skin.

He nuzzled her neck, nipping like the love-starved cowboy that he was. He gathered her backside in his hands and pulled her belly against his hips. She ground herself against him. The soft hair of her mound tickled his skin. He stroked upward, over the round of her hip, up the tender skin of her ribs to her breasts, soft heaven in his hands.

Low down, his pulse swelled against her. Just below her jaw, he pressed his mouth to her pulse, licked it with his tongue. The pressure under his mouth drummed with the same beat as the one throbbing against Emma's belly.

The vows he had taken on his wedding day had all come to mean what they should. This woman was his, and no vengeance-seeking gunfighter would keep her from him.

Till death do us part they had each vowed. He prayed that it wouldn't happen tomorrow.

She should have known that the squeeze of Matt's work-worn fingers fondling her breasts would be a for-ever touch. For good or ill, he was making an eternal vow, pressing his mouth just over her heart. What a ninny she had been to believe she could sample this then go about her merry life without him.

She sighed his name—she thought so, anyway. Half dizzy and fully out of breath, she wasn't sure. All perception of life beyond this bed began to blur.

One thing was clear as spring water, though. Her decision to go to California had been right. Hadn't her life taken every turn just to end up at this moment?

She must have made a noise of some kind, for he answered with a moan caught somewhere between pain and pleasure. He slid his hands to her derriere in a caress that rippled up her spine.

Rugged hands circled her bottom. Eight fingers and two devastatingly possessive thumbs stroked her skin. With each flick of his thumb and squeeze of his fingers he bound her to him.

His weight shifted. Crisp thigh hair over hot lean muscle scraped her flesh. A prairie-scented lock of hair slipped from behind his ear and slid over her throat in a brown-sugar hug. He smelled like the land. A breath of turned earth and storm clouds tickled her nose.

Even though he had shaved only hours ago, the prickle of his beard tingled her chest when he kneaded his chin against it.

Matt lifted his head. He looked into her eyes with a gaze that shot clear to her heart. He had told her he loved her. The golden-amber glow in his eyes declared it once more.

"I wish we'd gotten around to this a bit sooner," he whispered. She couldn't find the voice to remind him that she had wanted to.

He must have seen the thought in her face. "I couldn't have you once or twice. What we're doing now, darlin', this binds us."

She touched his lips, halting his words. That sensual mouth that laughed more than it grimaced came down full on her nipple and he spoke his feelings again with the language of tongue and mouth.

If it had been possible for a woman's soul to flow out of her body and into a man, that's the way it would happen. If not for the constraints of the flesh, she would be right there, inside Matt's heart.

Truly, though, she didn't want to flee the confines of her flesh. She had never been touched like this, inside or out. Every kiss, every scrape and curl of his long, bold fingers made her want to open to him.

When his hand crept low on her belly, seeking her most intimate spot, she did. Cool air licked her private spot an instant before Matt's finger stroked it.

When she felt she might come apart with the pleasure, her man, her true husband, eased himself up on his elbow. He crawled over her and knelt between her thighs. He spread them wider. He glanced down, looking at her there, then into her eyes.

"You are my heart, Emma. Every blessed beat of it."

Had she ever seen a sight like her husband? It was a wonder that her heart didn't fly right out of her bosom.

What a vision he was, naked muscle gleaming in the golden glow of the lamp. From his lean hard thighs, spread slightly, to the flat plane of his belly, glistening in a fine sheen of sweat, he made her want to reach for him.

She lifted her arms. His hair sifted across his shoulders when he leaned toward her. He braced his arms, rippling with tension, one on either side of her. Lamplight turned the coarse hair on his forearms to russet flames.

He slipped inside her as though that's where he should have been all along. There was a pinch, not even worthy of being called pain, and then an overwhelming need to draw him farther inside herself.

He thrust deep, she arched her hips. Breathless, she gasped his name, smelled his flesh. She lifted her head to nip his shoulder, tasted salt on his skin. Hard and slick, he rocked against her womb. A wave crashed inside her. It washed pleasure from the point of their joining to her clenching fingers, then tumbled to the tips of her toes.

Maybe flesh was no barrier to souls after all.

Hadn't her wedding vows declared that the two shall become one flesh?

She had been a fool to believe that she and Matt could share the pleasure of their bodies for a short time and then skip through life as though not a blessed thing had changed.

What a relief to know that the vow "Until death do us part," would not happen by Hawker's hand.

Praise be that she had found the courage to leave everything behind and begin new with her husband.

Chapter Fifteen

A slow, naked stretch between the sheets made Emma feel purely decadent. Sunlight streamed through the window.

It was well past time to get up. Hours ago, the rooster had given the wake-up call, and for the first time ever she had ignored it. She had snuggled deeper into Matt's embrace and listened to the even draw of his breathing.

Morning chores could wait for today. If the men had late coffee and breakfast this one time, they wouldn't die of it.

Now, under a tangled pile of bedclothes, she stretched her arms wide and splayed her fingers over the sheets. Even though Matt was no longer in the bed, the scent of him lingered. Every inch of her flesh blushed with the scrape and caress of his touch.

Tomorrow or the next day she would pack up what she could, but this sun-drenched, filled-with-birdsong morning she was a bride. Life was sweet, with the scent of coffee that she had not brewed drifting across the hall and into the bedroom.

Along with the aroma of coffee came Matt's voice singing a low happy tune.

She flipped back the covers and padded naked to the wardrobe. She put on her robe with no nightgown beneath. It felt scandalous and wonderful next to her skin, even though, as a married woman, there was not a bit of scandal involved.

If there hadn't been a nip in the morning air, she might have walked as bare as she had been born through the house without a bit of shyness. Life as a married woman had come alive with possibilities that she had never dreamed of.

While she couldn't act on all of them right now, with her daughter recovering in the next room, she would fit in as many as possible. If it meant that laundry, cooking and gathering eggs went undone for now, all was well.

Knowing that they would soon put several states between them and Hawker made her feel at ease. Her marriage would last a lifetime and that brought a smile to her face. With all the good fortune falling about her shoulders she might never frown again.

She tiptoed across the hall, peered in at Lucy sleeping with an arm about each one of her pups. Reassured that the child was truly on the mend, she walked toward the kitchen.

Standing in the doorway, she watched Matt with his back toward her pouring a cup of coffee. His hair, free of his hat, lay loose over his shoulders. It glinted dark gold in a beam of sunshine stealing through the window. His shirt hung on a hook beside her apron, and his jeans hung low on his hips. His toes tapped the floor in time to the tune he hummed.

"I didn't know you were such a hand with the coffeepot," she said.

He turned with a smile and held out the steaming mug toward her.

"Morning, darlin'. I was about to deliver this to you in bed."

She walked toward him, letting the bodice of her robe gape open on purpose. Standing so close that not even the aroma of coffee could have slid between, she took the mug from his big steady fist.

"If I had known that, I would have stayed put."

His hand cupped the back of her head. He kissed her until she felt hot coffee dribble down her fingers.

"Ouch," she mumbled against his mouth.

He blew against her lips, took the mug and set it on the table. He sat in a chair and eased her down onto his lap.

"Have I told you this morning how much I admire you, Mrs. Suede?" He slipped both hands inside her robe, and she leaned into him. The tips of her breasts tightened on his calloused palms.

"Yes, but it must have been two hours ago."

Beneath the robe his fingers fondled a nimble trail down her spine. Marriage in the flesh was ever so much better than whispered gossip had accounted for.

"The boys gathered up some jerky and leftover dinner biscuits. They headed off to mend fences—ought to be gone for hours."

"Lucy's sound asleep," she answered. "Do we dare?"

Matt was a daring man, and strong. He lifted her easily and settled her over, down and around him. Her muscles clamped him in a most intimate embrace. He took her in the chair.

In the days to come, she wouldn't have her kitchen, with her big polished table and her thoroughly modern stove, but there was no reason they couldn't bring this chair.

Half an hour later, Matt grinned at her across the table while they sipped cold coffee.

"Mama…Papa…I'm hungry" came a faint voice not far off.

Lucy stood in the doorway on pale, thin legs, with only a slight wobble to them.

Matt scooped his baby up and settled her at the table. Emma grabbed the frying pan.

She'd fill that child with all the eggs, bacon and pancakes her healing body could hold.

Lands, if she wouldn't see to it that Lucy ate everything that her little belly would accept before they boarded the train.

The gun in Matt's hand barked out a shot. The can on the post chimed with the impact, then spun in the air.

That made six shots and six empty tins lying on the grass.

He hadn't lost any accuracy over the years, but his speed had slowed some. An onlooker wouldn't notice the difference, but the drag was there and it would cost him his life.

He reset the cans, then shot them off in quick succession. It would take hours out here, on the far side of the creek where his practicing wouldn't endanger anyone, to get to where he had once been.

He hadn't expected to ever use his quick draw again. It was a skill best forgotten by him and everyone else.

Life had a way of changing a man's expectations,

though. At the beginning of summer he wouldn't have chosen to be a married man, settled in a home built by his own hands. Now, with fall setting in, he'd face a bullet to keep that from changing.

Matt laid out a line of new cans, since the old ones had been blasted into a set of tin peepholes. It was easy enough to shoot down an empty can of beans. A man was another thing altogether.

He set his legs, knees slightly bent. He let his hands lie loose beside his hips, then drew the Colt from his holster with a quick hiss of metal on well-worn leather. Six shots cracked, echoing over the land. Six cans flipped in the air, tumbling and catching glints of sunshine as they fell.

Faster, but not fast enough. If he cut the sight off the tip of the gun barrel, it would make for a smoother glide against the leather and might give him the advantage he needed. No doubt Hawker's piece had long since been doctored that way.

A ring of sweat dampened the band of his hat. Moisture dripped down his forehead, so he wiped it with his sleeve.

"What are you doing?" Emma's voice sounded horrified.

She knew what he was doing—it was obvious. She must want admission from his own lips.

"Shooting cans off posts, darlin'. Just what it looks like."

He crouched and pivoted right, taking aim at a fat gray bug that sprang suddenly into the air from the prairie sod. Grass crunched under Emma's boots. She touched his elbow. The shot went wide.

"Why?" she asked, her tone flat.

He shoved his Colt back into the holster, turned and gripped her by the upper arms.

"You know why." Her face looked pale even though he felt her anger rising. Best face this head-on and get it done with. "We're not getting on that train."

"Yes, we are, all of us." As she built a head of steam, her breath came hard and fast. "I told you I'm ready to go!"

"And that means everything to me." He loosened his grip on her arms and stroked them, the way he might calm a skittish mare. "But I know how you love this place."

Not being a mare, she was only made furious by his soothing. She twisted away from him.

"You don't know anything, Matthew Suede!" She backed away with the fingers of one hand pressed to her lips, then swept her skirt along with a snap. "It's you that I love. How happy do you think I'll be in my house knowing it caused your death? I'd hate every stick and board. I'd leave, anyway."

"There are some things a man can't run away from."

"I can run away." She turned her back to him. "I'll take Lucy and we'll move west by ourselves. I started once…I can do it again."

"Emma." He touched her shoulder. "You said you would stand by me no matter what."

"I never guessed that you meant this." With a sharp turn she slashed her arm at the cans littering the ground. "I'll follow you to hell, Matt, but don't ask me to weep over your grave."

A lark's song broke the silence that ached between them. In his mind he saw her doing just that, but it didn't change what he had to do.

"Unless I face Hawker now, that's how it will be. Maybe not here or now, but somewhere. And it's not just me anymore. Now that he knows about you, Lucy and Red, no one is safe." He wanted to hold her and convince her it was true, but her resentment burned too hot. "He'll follow us wherever we go."

"If we stay, you'll die." She leaned toward him, but didn't take a step. "I met the man. He'll kill you and then apologize to me for the inconvenience."

Silence again. He couldn't deny that might happen.

"I couldn't bear it, Matt."

With a twirl of blue calico, she spun away and ran toward home.

A feathery cloud spread thin over the sky, dimming the sunshine. Matt picked up the cans and set them back on the fence.

Lucy, while still weak, had begun to show a blush of pink in her cheeks. Already her eyes sparkled with returning health.

Emma sat with her on the porch, rocking under the warmth of a blanket and watching a bank of rain clouds roll in with the sunset.

From across the creek, she listened to the crack of Matt's gun. The ominous firing had gone on for hours without a letup. His relentless practice made her skin prickle with dread.

There was nothing she could do to change his mind. Not reason, not anger, not even giving up what meant the most. She had lied when she had told Matt she would leave this house no matter what. If all that was left of him was this place born of his sweat and his blisters, she would never leave it.

Lucy snuggled against Emma's breast, then popped her thumb out of her mouth.

"Mama, when I was sick I heard my heart talk to me."

"Did you now, and what did your heart say?" She stroked a web of fine blond curls away from Lucy's forehead, but they sprang right back into place.

"Drink the icky tea so I would get better and you could be my mommy forever."

Her heart constricted under her corset. Mercy, had the child turned back from the grave for a mother's love? Looking back at her own past, Emma knew she would have done it, too, had she ever been given that chance.

Chilly wind pushed the storm closer to the homestead and swirled the dust in the yard into puffs and sooty streaks. She wrapped the blanket a little tighter and hugged Lucy close to her chest. The shared warmth and mingled breath made her want to sit so forever.

"I wanted you to be my real mommy, so I drank it even though it tasted bad." She popped her thumb back into her mouth. Her babylike fingers brushed over Emma's heart with the rhythm of her sucking.

"Your heart spoke true, sweetie. I love you as much as any mother ever loved her little girl."

How could she not have known it from the very first day?

If the worst happened to Matt or if it didn't, this child was hers.

Rain slapped the bedroom window, carried by a sidelong wind. Emma bent her forehead to the glass and felt the beat of it. Even though the storm turned the yard to muck, which would end up on her floors, she was grateful for it.

A gunfight couldn't happen in a downpour.

Earlier, Matt had come in from his quick-draw practice just a few paces ahead of the storm. Not a word had passed between them in the hours since.

Emma touched the glass. She traced the zigzag trail of a drip of water. It looked like a giant teardrop.

Anger had made her a fool tonight. How she regretted telling Matt to sleep in the dugout with Red and Billy.

In a world that seemed suddenly out of control, this might be the one thing she could change. She dashed out of her room, down the hall and out the front door into the night before she realized that she had forgotten to put on a robe or shoes. Cold mud squished between her toes, but she pressed on toward the sod house. She banged on the door. "Matt!" she cried.

The door opened and she threw her sodden self into his arms.

"I'm sorry," she sobbed. "I will stand by you.... Please come home."

Red sat up in his bed, rubbing his hands over his hair. "What's going on?" he mumbled.

"Go back to sleep," Matt said and closed the door. He swept her up and ran through the downpour, back to the house.

Matt made love to his wife three times, each time intended to be an eternal vow. He longed to smash the clock in the hall, its relentless tick reminding him that there was nothing eternal about this night.

Rain pummeled the roof and flew against the windows. Under the covers, Emma faced him pressed tight to his side. Her breath, puffing warm against his neck, smelled sweet.

The even rise and fall of her ribs didn't fool him into thinking she was asleep. "Emma, we need to talk," he whispered.

She shook her head, then turned toward the window. The warmth of her round behind snuggled into his crotch.

"Some things have to be said…to be arranged."

"Unless you are going to tell me you are the fastest gun that ever lived and I don't have a thing to worry about, don't say a word…. I won't hear anything else." She tucked one hand under her cheek and reached back to rest her other hand on his hip. The movement pivoted her back so that her breast pointed up. He watched it jiggle with her heartbeat.

She was as frightened as he was. He could nearly hear her heart thumping through her skin.

He covered her breast with his hand, to still and comfort her. He brushed his fingers slowly over the plush mound, not in passion but hoping to still the quivering.

It didn't help much, given that his hand was no steadier than her heart.

Come morning, quaking like that would get him killed.

Some things had to be sorted out no matter the pain of saying them out loud.

With dawn, he'd have to close everything out of his mind but the slide of metal against leather. Until this job was done there would be no home, no children, no Emma.

Things had to be spoken now. Tomorrow, a single

thought or feeling that didn't have to do with shooting Hawker would be the nail shutting his coffin closed. A single loose string at home might mean his end.

"I can't say that." He turned her over, ran his thumb alongside her cheek. "That's why I need some promises from you."

She shook her head in denial but said, "All right. Tell me what to do to make you come back to me."

"I need to know that you and Lucy and Red are safe, here at home. If I think that you aren't I'll be distracted. Promise me you will stay here. No matter what, you'll keep everyone here."

"I promise, just as long as you don't tell me goodbye. Matt, never tell me goodbye."

"Why would I? I'll be home before dark, you'll see." All of a sudden the front door flew open with a force that knocked it back against the wall.

"Hope everybody's decent." Billy's voice boomed down the hall. "I'm coming in!"

A second later his big frame filled the doorway.

"Red's missing and so is his horse. I think he's gone to Dodge." Billy's voice sucked in and out of his lungs. "Jesse caught him in town a few nights ago ready to call out Hawker. I took his gun away and hid it, but it's gone now, too."

Chapter Sixteen

Nighttime in Dodge seemed the same in any weather.
Rowdy tunes plinked out of open saloon doors, men
laughed and argued, cards shuffled and chips chinked
on tables. Driving rain or sweltering night made no difference in the buzz of activity.

Life on Front Street seemed as normal as peas even
though the tension in Matt's gut nearly doubled him up.

During the charge from the homestead to town the
rain had slowed to a steady drizzle, but the wind howled
and swirled.

Cold mist covered his face in a clammy sheet. Lan-
terns squeaked on hooks up and down the boardwalk.
Their sway shot beams of light over the muddy street,
then twisted them back to stab jumpy lines on the
boardwalk again.

"I'll ride toward the livery," Billy said, rising in
the stirrups then resettling his weight. "We could use
Jesse's help."

Matt settled his soggy hat on his head. It wasn't much
cover, but it helped to slow the trickle of rain seeping
under his shirt.

"Cousin, if we part ways tonight, take care of my family." Emma would be grieved to hear that kind of talk, but the ride to town had turned his fingers stiff with cold. If he were forced to face Hawker like this, he would lose.

"Hey now, it won't come to that. But if it sets your mind at ease, I've got your back." Billy turned his horse toward the livery. Its hooves sucked at the muddy street, slowing what needed to be quick action.

Everything about tonight seemed slowed by the weather. Hawker was likely inside somewhere, keeping his shooting finger warm and swift.

"Where are you, Red?" Matt whispered even though he wanted to shout.

Thoughts of Emma crowded his brain, filled his senses. He closed his eyes, breathed in the moist night air and looked at the images of her behind his eyelids for the length of a sigh. Then he put her away.

Without success, he tried to call up the rash young man he had been, with no ties but the one between his hand and his weapon. That boy was gone, and in his place a husband and father, dead set on protecting what was his own.

He felt his determination swell, but also his vulnerability.

"Come on, boy," he murmured to Thunder. "Not enough ruckus in the saloon to let on that a green kid is inside calling out a gunfighter. Chances are Red is hiding out behind one of these buildings watching for Hawker."

Matt hunched his shoulders against the chill and rode a block to the land office. Red knew of the hiding place behind it from their bank-robbery days. It was a logical place for him to be now.

Nothing seemed amiss at first sight. Matt slid off the saddle and tied Thunder's reins to a bush.

He strode a few steps away from the horse, then stopped to listen. The night sounds that used to strike him as lively and exciting during his trail days now seemed tawdry.

Over the whiskey-primed laughter and the shuffle of the wind he strained to hear the voice of a boy who was too young to know that courage was not enough to triumph over a bullet. Red's adolescent sense of honor would plant him in the grave unless Matt found him soon.

He tucked his right hand under his armpit and hurried in the direction of the mercantile, his breathing shallow so that the hiss wouldn't cover the sound of trouble he was listening for.

Slowly his fingers warmed under his arm. Not enough to give him an advantage over a man who had been inside all evening, but with any luck, Hawker had been drinking.

"Punk—" The single word barked out from the south, the direction he was headed. The rest of what the voice said blew away in the wind.

Matt took three long strides with mud slick beneath his boots and then heard, "I'm not too young to put a hole through you!"

Damn! Red's voice, high-pitched and flushed with excitement, came from a few buildings down. He'd never get there in time.

Matt raced for the boardwalk. Mud-caked footwear

slid on the wet wood. He scrambled for balance, then ran past the bank. His boots sounded slow and muffled.

His heart whomped against his ribs in anticipation of a gunshot.

The shot cracked the instant he scooted into the alley that bordered the mercantile. He saw Red standing at the rear of the building. Smoke circled the tip of his gun.

Matt reached for his weapon on the run.

"It's a fool thing to want to die so young," an unseen stranger's voice said.

Reaching the corner of the building, Matt spotted the man who must be Hawker, shaking his head, looking almost sorrowful. In spite of the regret, he lifted his firearm, taking aim at Red's chest.

Red should have fired again but he stood still, paralyzed by fear.

"Hawker!" Matt yelled, skidding in the mud a few feet in front of Red. Fingers that needed to be flexible felt like frozen twigs.

Hawker fired his gun.

The impact of the bullet knocked Matt back and to his knees. Fire flashed through his arm, from shoulder to wrist. His hand turned useless. Stiff fingers dumped his Colt into the mud.

He glanced behind him, but Red was dazed and continued to stand as he was, his gun fallen nose-first into the muck at his feet.

"Run, boy!" Even Matt's voice felt on fire.

"Whoa here!" Hawker strode forward, his posture confident with easy victory. "Looks like I've got me two for the price of one."

He kicked Matt's gun away with his muddy boot toe.

"Let the boy go, Hawker. He's just a kid."

"Your kid, is he?" Hawker wiped the rain off his nose with his sleeve. "Seems to me I'll kill him first, just so you know what it feels like to lose someone."

He lifted the gun and sighted it, dead center on Red's chest.

Red's piece was only two feet behind Matt, but it might have been a mile.

Hawker gave an ugly half-faced smile. Matt lunged aiming his wounded shoulder, the one closest to the killer, at the man's knees.

Hawker's arm swung down. Matt felt the scrape of cold metal against his neck. His shoulder exploded in pain when it slammed into Hawker's leg.

A shot echoed between the buildings.

Hawker's knees hit the ground. His gun rocked in the crook of his finger before it smacked into the mud. With blank eyes, he crumpled on top of it.

Rain crashed down as though someone had sliced open a cloud.

Matt crawled toward the dead man. He knelt beside him, cradling his own wounded arm and feeling the warm rush of blood.

Water blended with blood under Hawker's chest. One lifeless eye filled with mud. The other stared out at the night, no longer seeing it.

Matt took off his hat and covered Hawker's face. He glanced about, searching the dark for the person who had fired the shot. There was only silence and rain.

Matt tried to stand but couldn't. He felt sick to his stomach and growing weak.

It was Red, though, coming out of his shock, who knelt on the ground retching his guts out.

There seemed to be voices gathering, coming from

high and low, swimming around his head in excited exclamations. Darkness weighted his limbs. It smothered his thoughts and choked out the light until he was nothing.

The hours of dark stretched longer than the hours of light. Every horror that a body imagined seemed true.

The steady pelt of rain made it that much worse.

Emma paced in front of the parlor window. She wore the shine off the hallway floor. She cracked open Lucy's bedroom door for the fifth time that evening. She forced her bottom down into the rocking chair, but sat with her feet flat and her spine straight. She stared at the front door, willing it to open.

And she listened. This house was full of unsettling sounds that she had never noticed before. Wood creaked. Hot metal from the stove popped as it cooled. Wolves on the prairie howled their wet misery, making the horses whinny in the barn.

But the one sound that she strained to hear would not come. Listen as she might, hoofbeats returning home seemed as far from her ears as town itself.

At eleven o'clock her stomach ached over the danger Matt was riding into. At midnight she felt he was dead. The certainty of it made her weep against the parlor window.

At one o'clock Lucy got out of bed looking for a drink of water.

Now with sunrise only a couple of hours away, she'd give anything to get on Pearl and go to town. The reality of what might be going on could hardly be worse than what she imagined.

Only the promise that she had made Matt kept her

here. The promise and the fact that she couldn't leave Lucy alone.

Heartsick at watching for the door to open, Emma got out of the rocking chair and sat back down on the sofa.

She faced the window in the dress she had put on as soon as Matt had left, needing to be ready for any emergency. She watched for sunrise even though she wouldn't be able to see it with the bank of rain clouds riding low over the land. Hopefully, daybreak would make her fears manageable.

Everyday chores would be her salvation. She ought to get some sleep in the next couple of hours, but every time she closed her eyes, she saw Matt drawing his gun, but too slowly because she had gotten angry with him during his practice.

Matt's draw was quick. She'd seen his hands, swift as anything, aiming his Colt and shooting cans off the fence. She'd also seen Hawker catch his hat right out of the wind.

If the worst had happened to Matt or to Red, surely Billy would have raced home to tell her.

That thought made such sense that she hung on to it. She thought it over and over until it didn't hurt to sit and breathe.

After a while her eyes felt as heavy as her heart. She must have slept for a moment, for when the front door crashed open and Red stumbled in, she bounded off the couch, startled and disoriented.

Only a second before, her dream had put her in Matt's arms, giving him a welcome-home kiss.

"What's happened?" she cried.

Through the open front door she saw Thunder standing beside the front porch, winded from an obviously difficult run. His head hung low and steam curled up from his damp hide.

Red was alone. "Where's Matt?"

The boy looked everywhere but in her eyes.

"Say something!" She turned his face. "Where is he?"

A sudden gasp seemed to come out of Red's gut rather than his lungs. He covered his face with dripping hands, then collapsed to his knees.

"It's all my fault!" he wailed. "This never would have happened except for me!"

"Oh, my Lord!" Emma's knees went weak. She slipped down beside Red. She touched his hair where the rain had matted it to his forehead.

She touched his fists. He resisted her attempt to gently draw them down, so she yanked.

His face, a mass of crimson blotches, showed his misery. His eyes peered out at her through bloodshot slits, made puffy from apparent weeping.

"He's dead?"

"Not yet." He hiccupped. "Just shot in the shoulder. But Pendragon and Bart both claim that Matt killed Hawker in cold blood. Say they witnessed it firsthand. That Matt plugged him while he was on the ground pleading for his life."

Once again Red covered his face and sobbed. Emma shook him by the shoulders.

Screaming and weeping would feel fine right now. How she longed to toss her head back and howl her despair like the wolves on the prairie did, but such a scene would only throw the situation out of control.

"You tell me everything that happened, young

man, and don't leave anything out." Her voice, at least, sounded composed. That would do for a start.

"I found Hawker coming out of the saloon. I followed him. Then, when nobody was about but me and him, I called him out." Red's voice steadied. He straightened his shoulders. "He laughed at first, but then I called him a yellow coward. We went around back of the mercantile. He called me a fool, punk, kid and I got so hot-mad that I drew my gun."

Red wiped his face with his sleeve. "Guess I am a fool kid. I got so riled that I shot wide. Hawker stood there with his shot unfired, aiming his gun at me and I...I couldn't even move!

"He meant to kill me, even though he seemed like maybe he didn't want to. Just then Matt came running between the buildings and yelled. He stood in front of me, saving my life while I just stood there too scared to move.

"Matt could have taken him easy, but he was off balance from slipping in the mud. That's when Hawker got him in the shoulder. Hawker thought to kill me first to make Matt suffer, but Matt knocked him with his hurt shoulder and then a shot came out of somewhere and killed Hawker on the spot."

"Praise be, Matt's safe and so are you. Only Hawker's dead."

"For now. Pendragon's pushing the marshal to yank Matt out of Doc Brown's office and hang him right after sunup."

"They won't hang him for defending you." Emma took a deep breath and closed her eyes, trying to sort things out in her mind. Matt was alive and Hawker was not. For the moment that's all that mattered.

"Not in a regular town, maybe. But you know how the marshal sits in Pendragon's pocket."

She'd think of a way out of this as soon as her insides quit spinning.

"Where's Billy?" She had nearly forgotten about Matt's cousin in all the upheaval.

"He's with Matt at the doc's."

"I'm going to town." She stood up, pressing her palm against Red's shoulder. "I need you to care for Lucy."

"I'm sorry, Emma." He snuffled. "I only thought I could make everything right."

"Everything will be all right." Emma kissed the top of his head. "See if I don't bring Matt home."

She rushed outside and grabbed Thunder's reins. Steam still curled up from his neck and back. The poor beast had barely caught his breath.

She stared up at his tall back and firmed her resolve. The horse was much too big for her. She'd ridden him only sitting securely in front of Matt.

"Come on over here to the step, boy. I can't quite reach the stirrup."

It was a stretch, but she made it up onto his broad saddle. She leaned forward, toward his flicking ear. "I wouldn't ask this of you, but it's Matt's life."

The horse lunged forward. It was all Emma could do to hold on. Maybe Thunder understood the urgency. Pearl would have. Even without knowing words, she felt things.

"Good horse," she whispered, hanging tight to a bolt of lightning.

Chapter Seventeen

Morning sunlight slanted through the lace curtains beside the recovery bed in Doc Brown's office. With his thumb, Matt traced the lacy pattern that it cast on the blanket. At home, the sun would be doing the same through Emma's curtains.

He half wished he hadn't made her promise to stay put, but some things were for the best. For all that he'd give a lifetime to see her smile, what he would see is her grief. Hanging was not something that a woman should see her husband do.

What he needed now was a song, but even if he could dig deep enough to find the notes, bringing them up would hurt like the devil.

At least he wasn't dead, not yet.

Billy strode in with a cup of coffee and sat in a chair beside the bed.

"Doc says you can't have any," he said. "At least for a while."

"In a while I'll be hanged," Matt grumbled. "Pass it over here."

"If I believed that, I would." Billy took a long swallow. "Guess you'll have to just smell it."

"I'm going home." Matt sat up and swung his legs over the edge of the bed. The image of Emma's smile was becoming irresistible, and as yet he wasn't under arrest.

The room spun like a lasso twisting through the air. The next thing he knew Doc Brown was bent over the bed telling him he was too weak to do anything but lie still.

"Hell." Matt pushed himself up with his elbows until the room settled enough to feel like nothing more challenging than a rocking boat. "I'm going home to kiss my wife goodbye."

"There will be no goodbyes, young man, as long as you follow doctor's orders." The doctor eased him up so that he reclined against a pair of pillows.

He felt as if he might be sick, but the dizziness passed in a moment.

"I wasn't the one who shot Hawker, Doc. But Pendragon will make sure I hang for it, anyway. Might as well give me some coffee and send me home."

"You didn't see anything?" Billy asked one more time.

"I saw my life pass before my eyes."

Doc Brown snatched the coffee cup from Billy and took a deep swallow. "I always wondered about—"

The door to the front office opened, then banged closed. Arguing voices carried through the walls.

Doc Brown mumbled something about no respect for the sickroom and marched toward the door that separated the rooms. He had to jump back when it flew open and Lawrence Pendragon charged in with Bart close on his heels.

Marshal Deeds followed seconds later with a scowl on his face.

"See here, Marshal." Doc Brown ignored Pendragon and Bart, lodging his protest with the lawman. "This is a sickroom. You can't come barging in."

"You've got a killer in your bed, Dr. Brown," Pendragon said, his sneer mean to the core. "You wouldn't want it known that you are harboring a fugitive. That's illegal, is it not, Mr. Deeds?"

Billy jumped up with his fist clenched. "Matt's no criminal and you know it."

"I know for a fact that he is." Pendragon's fancy clothes smelled of nicotine when he moved. His grin bore the stains of his habit. "So does Bart. We both witnessed Mr. Suede gun down a man in cold blood."

"Hawker was pleading for his life," Bart put in. "Groveling in the dirt with his hands over his face and weeping like a woman. Didn't make no never mind to Suede, though. He plugged him, anyway. Yes, sir, then he laughed in the dead man's face. Told him to go to hell."

"Pendragon," Matt said, swinging his legs over the side of the bed. He stood up even though he didn't know if his legs could do what his mind ordered, but hell would freeze over before he'd face these accusations sitting down.

"You're lying because you want my land," Matt said. Billy stood beside him, shoulder touching shoulder so that Matt could stand tall without being held up. "Bart was probably too drunk to know a thing that you didn't pay him to know."

"Marshal," Pendragon ordered. "Take this man into custody. We can see justice done within the hour."

"Whooeee!" Bart scraped his nose across his sleeve, grinning and giggling. "The noose has barely quit swinging from yesterday."

The marshal stood still. He glared from Bart to Pendragon and back with his arms folded across his chest.

"Suede is in no condition to face justice."

"I hardly see what difference it makes, Marshal." Pendragon reached for Matt.

Marshal Deeds stepped between Matt and Pendragon's reaching fist. "I'll take charge of my own prisoner."

For half a heartbeat the land baron's eyes widened. Then they narrowed, glaring menace. "Do your duty, then."

"My patient shouldn't be moved!" Doc Brown appealed to the marshal.

"Shut up, old man," Bart snarled. "He ain't your patient no more."

The marshal took Matt's good arm with more support than force and led him toward the front door.

"Mighty sorry, Suede," he mumbled so low that Matt figured he had heard wrong.

Pendragon marched in the lead. Red faced, he opened the front door and let it slam against the wall. Maybe he wasn't used to the marshal trying to wriggle out from under his thumb.

Matt had to blink against the sudden glare of daylight as sunshine glinted off a colorful group of people strutting and puffing up the street. Bonnets and feathers, cowboy hats and derbies bounced with their long strides.

Calico-clad ladies brushed elbows with satin draped

ladies of the night. Merchants and farmers marched together. Damned if they weren't followed by the bankers.

He must be sicker than he thought to bring on this
hallucination. He closed his eyes, willing the bizarre
scene to go away, but soon he heard the grumble of the
crowd coming closer.

Grumble?

He had expected to hang, but not at the hands of a
brightly hued lynch mob.

Footsteps rushed up the porch steps, tapping lightly
on the wood. A hand stroked his cheek. Gentle fingers
touched his sling from injured shoulder to protruding
fingertips

If this was a trick of the mind, he gave himself up
to it.

He felt his head being lowered by a pair of tender
hands near his ears. Petticoats rustled as though the
wearer had risen to her toes. A pair of lips touched his.

"Emma?" Did he dare open his eyes and ruin the
hallucination?

She hugged him around the middle and it hurt. Great
blessed pain! "Emma!"

He pulled her in tight with his good arm, trying to
make the feel of her last forever, but the mob did sound
angry.

They looked angry, too, waving fists, farming tools
and even a few bottles of…Orange Lilly? And they were
headed straight for Doc Brown's front porch.

Red faced and beginning to sweat, Marshal Deeds
stepped back a few paces.

"You were supposed to stay home," Matt whispered
in Emma's ear.

"You were supposed to come home," she whispered back.

"Free Suede! Free Suede!" the group of more than fifty folk began to chant.

Faces that he recognized, and some that he didn't, moved close to the bottom step. Emma ran her hands lightly over his shoulder, looking for damage. She'd find it, for sure, but his strength seemed to be returning by the second.

"Where did all these folks come from?"

"Cowboys aren't the only ones capable of a roundup. I told some of them what was happening, then they told some others and here we are."

Watching the Sizeloffs move forward gave him the strength to stand unaided. Jesse and his girl, flanked by Mr. Rath and Mr. Wright, made the ache in his shoulder ease. The sight of Woody, Sarah and Lenore Pendragon moving toward the front of the crowd gave him hope.

The ladies of the Long Branch, looking as colorful as a flock of tropical birds, made him a little nervous. He glanced at his wife. If Emma or anyone else was offended by their presence it didn't show.

The anger, and there was plenty of it, seemed to be directed at the marshal, Pendragon and Bart.

"Marshal!" Pendragon roared. "Do something about this!"

"Throw 'em all in jail." Bart waved his hand at the group, but lost his balance and rolled down the steps.

"What do I pay you—" All of a sudden Pendragon shut his mouth. He stared for a moment at the sunlight glinting off the toe of his boot. "Do what you have been elected to do."

The marshal looked at Matt, then at Pendragon's

twitching mustache. He shook his head and swallowed hard. Sweat beaded Deeds's forehead.

"Marshal Deeds." Rachael Sizeloff touched his sleeve, inviting him down the steps. "A word with you, please."

When Pendragon made a move to stop him, Joseph Sizeloff muscled between them, giving his wife the opportunity to lead the marshal across the street.

From this distance Matt couldn't hear the private conversation, but some things didn't need words. Rachael held baby Maude in one arm while gesturing with the other.

Head hung low, the marshal listened to the minister. He looked a bit green when she frowned and pointed a firm finger toward the dirt, shaking her head. After that, Deeds seemed to have a few things to say. He talked for a while, sometimes covering his eyes, sometimes wringing his hands. All the while the preacher nodded. When Deeds quit speaking, Mrs. Sizeloff gave him a brilliant smile and pointed toward the sky.

The marshal looked like a different man, being led back across the street and up the steps. Like a man relieved of a burden.

Pendragon, though, looked like a bull ready to charge. Only a severe scowl from Joseph Sizeloff held him in his place.

On the top step of the porch and gazing over the crowd, Marshal Deeds twisted his hat in his hands.

"I have something to confess to all of you good people," he announced. Rachael beamed up at him, looking as proud as a mother hen. "Matthew Suede didn't kill anyone. I did."

Pendragon made a leap toward Deeds, but Woody

Vance raced up the steps. Joseph and Woody restrained him with one arm looped through each of his.

"I shot him in the line of duty when he was about to kill Matt and his boy. The only wrong done is to the citizens of this town, by me. I've been influenced by power...and money."

Every eye in the silent crowd focused on Lawrence Pendragon, who curiously looked a few inches shorter.

"So I resign." Deeds took off his badge, looked about for someone to hand it to, then pressed it into the fist of Doc Brown. "I ask your forgiveness before I leave town."

With a backward glare at Pendragon, he went down the steps. Mrs. Sizeloff caught his sleeve as he passed.

"Go with God, Mr. Deeds," she said.

"Well." Doc Brown spoke to the murmuring crowd. "It appears we need a new lawman."

"Billy Suede would be a fine choice," Woody Vance called out.

Sarah beamed up from the foot of the steps. "Billy! Oh yes, now there's a man who can be trusted."

Murmers of Billy's name went from the front of the group to the back.

"I cast my little bitty vote for Billy Suede," Lulu Frolic sang out, with feathers and satin bouncing.

Six pairs of red-tipped hands shot into the air. "Oooh, so do we!"

Giggles twittered. The ladies swept sideways together, their colors a moving rainbow. They circled Bart, who had been creeping toward the edge of the crowd.

"You vote for Billy, don't you, Bart?" Lulu asked.

"Sure, honey, whatever you say." He looked as nervous as a bug cornered by a flock of hens.

"What I say," Lulu announced, "and we all do, is thanks for the vote and you might as well leave town with Mr. Deeds because there won't be a drop of anything for you at the Long Branch or anywhere else!"

He backed slowly away while they shooed their skirts at him.

"I meant to leave here, anyway," he grumbled. When Lulu took a step forward and clapped her hands in his face, he turned and ran, kicking up mud clods until he was out of sight.

"So, who else votes for Billy?" Doc Brown raised the badge in the air.

Every hand shot up except Lawrence Pendragon's.

"Well, Billy, do you accept the position?"

Billy took the badge from the doc and pinned it on his shirt. When he rubbed it to a shine with his sleeve, a cheer went up.

"Marshal Suede." Matt beamed at his cousin. "Is my wife free to take me home?"

Another cheer. Life's road stretched before him with love and laughter at every mile.

"Not until later," the doctor warned, looking at Emma and ignoring his protests altogether. "He's healing well, but wait until sundown just to make sure there's no fever."

"We'll stay." Emma tucked her strong little body beneath his good shoulder and turned Matt toward the door.

"Marshal Suede." Pendragon, now free of his captors, blocked the doorway.

If the land baron had been looking at Emma instead

of scowling at the new marshal, he'd have seen her solid little boot toe coming for his shin. Instead he doubled over and grabbed his leg.

Laughter twittered through the crowd until the man opened his mouth again.

"I demand that you lock up Matthew Suede for bank robbery. He's The Ghost and everyone here knows it!"

"Father!" Lenore Pendragon rushed up the porch steps. A good-size crowd had now gathered on the small veranda. If anyone else had something to say, they would have to do it from below.

Young Lenore placed her hands on her hips and raised her brows at her father. "Perhaps you would like to take a walk with Preacher Sizeloff, as well."

"Lenore Emily Pendragon, I order you to go home without another word." He faced his offspring, teeth gritted and short of breath. A nerve in his eye jumped in time with a tic in his cheek.

"Well, then, if you won't come clean, I'll have to do it for you."

Lenore arched her eyebrows, fluffed her expensive skirt and told every eager ear the sorry tale of Lucy's father's death and how her own father had neglected the child's welfare.

"And so," she finished, "I had no choice but to become The Ghost."

Even the bird chirruping on the roof fell silent.

"Someone had to take responsibility for the child," Lenore said. When her father looked stunned enough to be pushed over with an accusing word, she added, "Marshal, do your duty."

She held out her hands, dainty wrists pressed together.

"There's no call to do that." Woody Vance puffed his chest, nodded at Matt and winked at Emma. "I'm The Ghost."

"No, I'm The Ghost," confessed Jesse, while his girl beamed her pleasure.

"So am I," insisted Mr. Sizeloff.

"We are, too!" a trio of farm wives called, each hoisting a bottle of Orange Lilly into the air.

Within a space of four minutes, no less than forty people had confessed to the crime. Only babes in arms had not.

Lawrence Pendragon's backside had sunk to the top step some moments past. He looked pale and green all at once.

Billy lifted his hands to still the murmers washing through the crowd.

"As marshal, I declare that since I can't arrest everyone, I won't arrest anyone." A cheer went up. "Let it be acknowledged by all that the ghostly spirit has finally passed on to his reward."

Matt knew he shouldn't be grinning, but he had passed to his reward, right here on earth. With Emma tucked here under his good arm, with Lucy on the mend and Red likely cured from his recklessness, he had everything he could ever want.

He was a rich man without money.

"One more thing needs to be made clear from the start. Most especially to you, Pendragon," Billy declared, crossing his arms over his chest. A wink of sunlight glanced off his badge. "Best look up at me while I'm speaking, just so we all know you understand. I'm not a lawman who can be bought. If you want something done in town it had better be legal and gone about like everyone else does. No more threats, no more scaring folks off their land."

If Matt had ever heard more cheering in one day he couldn't recall.

Billy sat on the step beside Pendragon and spoke in a low tone. "We all expect you to be a model neighbor. A body never knows when The Ghost might be resurrected."

Land sakes! What did a woman have to do to get her husband to listen to doctor's orders and rest? Dance naked at the foot of the bed?

Home could not come soon enough.

They should have remained in Dodge for another day, but Matt was not proving to be the most restful of patients. Only a wifely scowl had convinced him that she would be the one to drive the wagon home.

Emma licked the prairie dust from her lips. She jiggled the reins of the rented team and glanced sideways at Matt. He sat tall even with the pain in his shoulder, watching the golden land dim with the sunset.

A bird dipped low over her land singing to the departing day. Matt's land, too. He had earned his place here. Mercy, if he hadn't spilled his blood to protect it and those who lived here.

Without him, nothing on this 160 acres would mean a thing.

"What are you smiling about, darlin'?"

"Going home is against doctor's orders."

"Doc Brown worries too much."

"Good thing you've got me to keep you in line."

Emma laughed, feeling the joy of it to her toes and

back. "Don't look so stricken, Matt. I'll take such loving care of you that you won't even notice that wound."

And she knew that Matt would take loving care of her, as well. For the rest of their days there would be the two of them, watching over each other and tending the land.

In just one summer Matt had turned her notions of happiness upside down. On that first ride to her land she hadn't understood that a home was not just walls sticking up out of the earth. He had shown her that home was made of the souls living and laughing inside it.

While the blessings of home and hearth went bone deep, the blessings of family filled her soul.

Just now lights came into view, shining like a beacon across the darkening prairie.

The wheels of the buggy creaked across Suede land, bringing them closer to home. From behind, the rising moon illuminated the way.

From a hundred yards off she spotted Red and Lucy through the parlor window, sitting in the rocking chair together beside the fireplace. They were both laughing, watching Princess and Fluffy cavorting over the furniture.

Smoke curled out of the chimney, light against the now fully dark sky.

"We're home," she murmured.

Matt grinned at her and gave her a kiss.

Then he began to sing.

* * * * *

MONTANA BRIDE
Jillian Hart

Left widowed, pregnant and penniless, Willa Conner's last hope is the stranger who answers her ad for a husband. Austin Dermot, a hardworking Montana blacksmith, doesn't know what to expect from a mail-order bride. It certainly isn't the brave, beautiful, but scarred young woman who cautiously steps off the train...
(Western)

OUTRAGEOUS CONFESSIONS OF LADY DEBORAH
Marguerite Kaye

I am the Dowager Countess of Kinsail, and I have enough secrets to scandalize you for life. Only now I have a new secret, one that I will risk my life to keep: I am accomplice to Elliot Marchmont, gentleman, ex-soldier and notorious London thief. His touch ignites a passion so intoxicating that surviving our blistering affair unscathed will be near impossible....
(Regency)

A NOT SO RESPECTABLE GENTLEMAN?
Diane Gaston

Since returning to London, Leo Fitzmanning's kept his mind off a certain raven-haired heiress. Until he discovers that Miss Mariel Covendale is being forced into an unscrupulous marriage! Leo must re-enter the society he detests to help her, but soon there's *nothing* respectable about his reasons for stopping Mariel's marriage!
(Regency)

LADY WITH THE DEVIL'S SCAR
Sophia James

Badly disfigured Lady Isobel Dalceann has fought fiercely to defend her keep, with little thought for her safety—why, then, has she let a stranger within her walls? His battered body mirrors her own scars and tempts her to put her faith in him. But what would she do if she were ever to find out who Marc de Courtenay really is?
(Medieval)

REQUEST YOUR FREE BOOKS!

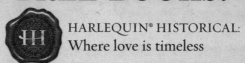

HARLEQUIN® HISTORICAL:
Where love is timeless

2 FREE NOVELS PLUS 2 **FREE GIFTS!**

YES! Please send me 2 FREE Harlequin® Historical novels and my 2 FREE gifts (gifts are worth about $10). After receiving them, if I don't wish to receive any more books, I can return the shipping statement marked "cancel." If I don't cancel, I will receive 6 brand-new novels every month and be billed just $5.19 per book in the U.S. or $5.74 per book in Canada. That's a savings of at least 17% off the cover price! It's quite a bargain! Shipping and handling is just 50¢ per book in the U.S. and 75¢ per book in Canada.* I understand that accepting the 2 free books and gifts places me under no obligation to buy anything. I can always return a shipment and cancel at any time. Even if I never buy another book, the two free books and gifts are mine to keep forever.

246/349 HDN FEQQ

Name   (PLEASE PRINT)

Address   Apt. #

City   State/Prov.   Zip/Postal Code

Signature (if under 18, a parent or guardian must sign)

Mail to the **Reader Service:**
IN U.S.A.: P.O. Box 1867, Buffalo, NY 14240-1867
IN CANADA: P.O. Box 609, Fort Erie, Ontario L2A 5X3

Not valid for current subscribers to Harlequin Historical books.

Want to try two free books from another line?
Call 1-800-873-8635 or visit www.ReaderService.com.

* Terms and prices subject to change without notice. Prices do not include applicable taxes. Sales tax applicable in N.Y. Canadian residents will be charged applicable taxes. Offer not valid in Quebec. This offer is limited to one order per household. All orders subject to credit approval. Credit or debit balances in a customer's account(s) may be offset by any other outstanding balance owed by or to the customer. Please allow 4 to 6 weeks for delivery. Offer available while quantities last.

Your Privacy—The Reader Service is committed to protecting your privacy. Our Privacy Policy is available online at www.ReaderService.com or upon request from the Reader Service.

We make a portion of our mailing list available to reputable third parties that offer products we believe may interest you. If you prefer that we not exchange your name with third parties, or if you wish to clarify or modify your communication preferences, please visit us at www.ReaderService.com/consumerschoice or write to us at Reader Service Preference Service, P.O. Box 9062, Buffalo, NY 14269. Include your complete name and address.

HHI1B

When Lady Deborah Napier blackmails notorious London thief Elliot Marchmont into becoming his accomplice, the thrill of adventure is *nothing* compared to the sudden rush of intoxicating passion that he incites within her….

"If I take you, it will be because I want to."

The words made Deborah shiver. Did he want her? Want *her?* No one had ever wanted her like that. "And do you—want me?"

Looking around swiftly to check they were quite alone, Elliot pulled her to him, a dark glint in his eyes. "You are playing a very dangerous game, Deborah Napier. I would advise you to have a care. For, if you dance with the devil, you are likely to get burnt. You may come with me, but only if you promise to do exactly as I say."

"You mean it!" *Oh God, he meant it!* She would be a housebreaker. A thief! "I'll do exactly as you say."

"Then prove it. Kiss me," Elliot said audaciously, not thinking for a moment that she would.

But she did. Without giving herself time to think, her heart hammering against her breast, Deborah stood on tiptoe, pulled his head down to hers and did as she was bid. Right there in Hyde Park, in the middle of the day, she kissed him.

She meant it as a kiss to seal their bargain, but as soon as her lips touched his, memories, real and imagined, made the taste of him headily familiar. His lips were warm on hers, every bit as sinfully delicious as she'd imagined, coaxing her mouth to flower open beneath his, teasing her lips into compliance, heating her gently, delicately, until his tongue touched hers.

It was a kiss like none she had ever tasted, heated by the

bargain it concluded, fired by the very illicitness of their
kissing here in a public space, where at any moment they
could be discovered. She could not have imagined, could
not have dreamed that kissing, just kissing could rouse her
in this way.

"Are you quite sure you want to do this?" he asked.

"Oh yes," she said, "I'm sure."

Elliot *always* gets what he wants. But will this most
accomplished thief steal his greatest prize to date—
Lady Deborah's heart?

Find out in
OUTRAGEOUS CONFESSIONS OF LADY DEBORAH
by Marguerite Kaye,
available from Harlequin® Historical in August 2012.

HHEXP0812